'Is there anyone I can call to come over and stay with you?' Ezra asked.

'I don't need anybody. I'll be all right.'

'You won't—and I don't just mean simply tonight. Jess, you're going to be in plaster for a minimum of eight weeks. You might just be able to do your surgeries but how are you going to do any home visits or night calls when you can't drive?'

'It's not your problem,' she pointed out.

'Of course it's my problem,' he flared. 'There's only one thing I can do. I'll have to stay.'

'Stay?' she echoed faintly.

'And not just for tonight,' he fumed. 'I'm going to have to stay with you until you get a locum.'

Maggie Kingsley says she can't remember a time when she didn't want to be a writer but she put her dream on hold and decided to 'be sensible' and become a teacher instead. Five years at the chalk face was enough to convince her she wasn't cut out for it, and she 'escaped' to work for a major charity. Unfortunately—or fortunately!—a back injury ended her career, and when she and her family moved to a remote cottage in the north of Scotland it was her family who nagged her into attempting to make her dream a reality. Combining a love of romantic fiction with a knowledge of medicine gleaned from the many professionals in her family, Maggie says she can't now imagine ever being able to have so much fun legally doing anything else!

Recent titles by the same author:

DR MATHIESON'S DAUGHTER
A WIFE FOR DR CUNNINGHAM
JUST GOOD FRIENDS
CHANGING LIVES

THE STRANGER'S SECRET

BY
MAGGIE KINGSLEY

MILLS & BOON®

First published in Great Britain 2002
Harlequin Mills & Boon Limited,
Eton House, 18-24 Paradise Road, Richmond, Surrey TW9 1SR

© Maggie Kingsley 2002

ISBN 0 263 17392 5

Set in Times Roman 10½ on 11 pt.
15-0402-53437

Printed and bound in Great Britain
by Antony Rowe Ltd, Chippenham, Wiltshire

CHAPTER ONE

'ARE you all right?'

The driver of the dark blue Mercedes wasn't simply a maniac, Jess decided, opening her eyes slowly, only to close them again when a searing pain shot down her leg. He was a gold-plated, top-of-the-class idiot as well. How on earth could she possibly be 'all right' after he'd just driven at breakneck speed round the corner of the single-track road straight into her car?

'I really don't think you should try to move,' the deep male voice continued with concern when she eased herself gingerly back from her steering-wheel. 'You might be injured.'

'Of course I'm injured,' she muttered through clenched teeth. 'My right leg's fractured.'

'It may simply be jarred—'

'I'm a doctor and, believe me, it's fractured.' And if I'm not very careful I'm going to burst into tears, Jess realised with dismay when a cool, firm hand suddenly enveloped hers.

She didn't need this. She really, *really* didn't need this. Five minutes ago she'd been congratulating herself on having got through all her afternoon home visits early. Had even thought she might actually have time to attack her mounting paperwork before the start of her evening surgery, and now...

'Are you in pain anywhere else?' the male voice said quickly as a sob came from her. 'Your chest, neck—'

'Look, do you suppose you could stop playing doctor for a moment and concentrate on getting me out of here?' she

5

asked as the fingers which had been taking her pulse moved to her throat.

'Wouldn't it be more sensible if I called for an ambulance?'

Good grief, the idiot was using the tone she always adopted when she was dealing with a difficult child. If she'd been fit enough she'd have hit him.

'There isn't any ambulance,' she said tightly. 'At least not today. It's down in the garage, having an overhaul.'

'Then another doctor—'

'There isn't another doctor on Greensay, only me.'

'I still don't think—'

'No, you obviously don't, do you?' she retorted, fighting back her tears. 'Because if you *had* thought you wouldn't have been driving like a maniac, and if you *hadn't* been driving like a maniac I wouldn't—'

'Be in this mess?' he finished for her awkwardly. 'Look, I'm really sorry. I needed a few things from the shops—'

'And you thought they might disappear unless you drove at eighty miles an hour?'

A low, husky chuckle was his only reply, and she turned towards the sound and tried to focus.

He was a tall man. That much she could see in the pale January moonlight. A tall man in his mid-thirties with deep grey eyes, thick black hair and a beard.

And she knew him.

Not to speak to. Nobody on the island knew him yet to speak to. But she'd seen him last week, walking along the beach the day after he'd moved into Sorley McBain's holiday cottage. Walking as though he had all the cares of the world on his shoulders.

'You're the drug dealer,' Jess murmured. 'The one who's lying low until the heat's off.'

'The drug...?' His fingers reached swiftly for her wrist again.

'That's what Wattie Hope reckons at any rate. Or an axe

murderer who's come to Greensay to dispose of the dis-
membered bits and pieces of your ex-wife.'

He sat back on his heels, his grey eyes glinting with
amusement. 'I see. And you—what do you think?'

'I'm just wondering if your car is as much of a write-off
as mine.'

'No, but, then, I don't drive a sardine can,' he replied,
gazing critically at her beloved little hatchback. 'Surely if
you're the only doctor on the island you should have cho-
sen something more substantial to drive.'

'Look, could we just stick to the point?' she returned
acidly. 'Is your car driveable?'

'The front bumper's bent, and the offside light and in-
dicator are smashed, but apart from that—'

'Then you can drive me to the Sinclair Memorial in
Inverlairg.'

The man's black eyebrows snapped down. 'I really don't
think—'

'You're doing it again—thinking—and I'd far rather you
didn't,' Jess interrupted. 'Now, are you going to help me
out of my car, or do I have to crawl?'

For a second he hesitated, then held out his hands to her.
Large hands, she noticed, strong hands. Which was just as
well, she realised, because when she tried to stand up another shaft of pain had her grabbing frantically at the front
of his Arran sweater.

'Care to reconsider your plan?' he said gently as she
buried her face in his chest, desperately fighting the waves
of nausea and pain which threatened to engulf her.

Actually, she'd have liked nothing better. Just to stand
here wrapped in this man's arms was infinitely preferable
to the thought of the journey ahead. And she was mad.
Good grief, he could have killed her and yet all she could
think as she clung to him was that he smelt of the sea, and
of warmth, and shelter.

'What I want,' she managed to reply, after taking several

deep breaths, 'is for you to stop talking, stop thinking and get me into your car.'

His mouth quirked into a rueful smile. 'Are you always this bloody-minded, Dr...Dr...?'

'Arden. The name's Jess Arden, Mr Dunbar.'

All amusement disappeared instantly from his face and his voice when he spoke was clipped, tight. 'You know me?'

'Not from Adam. Sorley McBain said he'd rented his cottage to an Ezra Dunbar from London—'

'A talkative man, Mr McBain.'

'You can't really blame him,' Jess replied defensively, hearing the decided edge in his voice. 'I mean, we get lots of people renting holiday cottages on Greensay in the summer—Americans mostly, looking for their Scottish roots—but it's pretty unusual for someone to take a cottage for three months in the middle of winter.' She glanced up at him with a slight frown. 'Does it bother you—people knowing your name?'

He didn't answer. Instead he slipped his arm round her waist, balanced her against his hip, then carried her across to his Mercedes. An action which left her white-faced and shaking, and feeling sick all over again.

'You know, your leg really ought to be splinted,' he observed after he'd pushed the front passenger seat of his car back as far as it would go. 'It's a ten-mile trip down to Inverlairg and no matter how slowly I drive you're going to get jolted. Perhaps I could find some pieces of wood to splint it—'

'And perhaps you could just let me worry about my leg?' Jess flared, driven beyond all endurance.

For a second she thought he was going to argue with her again, but by the time he'd eased her into the car Jess heartily wished she'd let him find those pieces of wood, and that he'd used them to knock her unconscious.

'Feeling rough?' he murmured sympathetically when he finally got into the driver's seat beside her.

'A bit,' she admitted, pushing back her damp hair from her forehead with a trembling hand.

He shook his head. 'I'm not surprised. Frankly, I don't know whether to admire you for your courage or condemn you for your stupidity.'

'While you're making up your mind, could you just drive?' she suggested, and he chuckled as he switched on his car's ignition.

'Regular little firebrand, aren't you? Goes with the red hair, I suppose. Your eyes wouldn't happen to be green, would they?'

They were, but Jess didn't feel up to acknowledging it as he turned his Mercedes in the direction of the town, or to informing him that she'd always been short-tempered even as a child. So he thought her a firebrand, did he? Well, right now she felt more like a damp squib. A squib that was giddy, and in pain, and more frightened than she'd ever been in her life.

What if she hadn't simply fractured her leg? What if she'd suffered internal injuries as well? She couldn't afford to be ill, couldn't so much as catch a cold, when it would mean leaving her patients with a two-and-a-half-hour ferry ride to the nearest doctor on the mainland.

'Why are you the only doctor on the island?' Ezra asked suddenly, as though he'd read her mind. 'Surely there's too much work here for you on your own?'

'Not for most of the time, there's not,' she answered, biting down hard on her lip as his car hit a pothole. 'Greensay only has a population of six hundred.'

'But those six hundred don't all live in the main town,' he argued back. 'From what I've seen, a lot of them live in outlying crofts, and if you're called out at night—'

'I manage,' she replied defensively. 'My father was the doctor here for thirty years before he died, and he managed.'

He glanced across at her, his grey eyes pensive. 'I see.'

She rather thought he saw more than she wanted him to.

That it hadn't simply been a desire to return to the island where she'd been born which had brought her back when her father had died three years ago. It had been a desire to follow in his footsteps, to be as good a doctor as he had been.

And why shouldn't she want that? she asked herself as they drove through the dark countryside. She'd adored her father, had always loved the island and its people. Why shouldn't she want to emulate him?

Yes, it was tough sometimes, being permanently on call. And, yes, there were days when she was so bone-weary it took all her strength to drag herself down to the health centre, but she couldn't have borne it if a stranger had taken over her father's practice. She had to succeed. She simply *had* to.

'Where do we go for the A and E unit?' Ezra asked when they finally arrived outside the imposing Edwardian building which housed the Sinclair Memorial Hospital.

'There isn't one as such,' Jess replied, sucking in her breath sharply as he carried her up the steps. 'But if you ring the bell at Reception Fiona should come.'

The staff nurse did, and the minute she saw them her face crumpled in dismay. 'Oh, my word…!'

'I'm OK, Fiona, honestly,' Jess interrupted quickly. 'I just took a corner too fast and landed in a ditch. I think I've fractured my right tibia—possibly my patella as well.'

'Not to mention having also acquired a very nasty bump on your forehead.' Fiona's eyes drifted towards Ezra. 'And you are…?'

'The drug dealer,' he replied blandly. 'Or the axe murderer—take your pick.'

'Ezra Dunbar!' she exclaimed triumphantly. 'You've taken Sorley McBain's holiday cottage—'

'For the next three months.' He nodded with resignation. 'Yes, that's me.'

'Well, thank goodness you did,' Fiona declared, lowering Jess carefully into a wheelchair, then pushing her through a door marked X-RAYS. 'We islanders don't tend to go out much in the evening in winter and heaven knows how long Jess might have been stuck in her car if you hadn't happened along.'

'I didn't exactly happen—'

'Would you mind staying with Jess until I get Bev and Will?' Fiona continued. 'I won't be a minute.'

And before either of them could reply she was gone in a flurry of starched green cotton.

'Bev is our part-time radiographer,' Jess explained as a frown creased Ezra's forehead. 'Will's her husband, and a first-rate anaesthetist, though how long we'll be able to keep him is anybody's guess. Our resident surgeon retired last year, you see, and we haven't been able to replace him. I can do some surgery, but—'

'Why did you do that?'

'Do what?' she asked in confusion.

'Tell her the accident was your fault?'

Jess eased herself gingerly round in her wheelchair. 'I don't think you'd have a very happy three months here if word got round that you're the man who trashed the doctor's car and landed her in hospital.'

The frown deepened. 'But why should you care? Like you said, you don't know me from Adam.'

She was hurting more and more by the second, and was in no mood to try to explain what she didn't quite understand herself, but she managed to dredge up a smile. 'Maybe I'm an old softy at heart. Maybe I'm just too sore to be able to think straight.'

'Yes, but—'

'Didn't I tell you to buy a decent car—well, didn't I?' Will Grant declared as he breezed into the X-ray department. 'Buy a Volvo or a Range Rover, I said—'

'Yes, we all know what you said, dear,' his wife Bev interrupted, pushing past him, 'and right now I don't suppose Jess wants to hear you repeat it. Fractured right tibia and patella, you reckon?' she continued, eyeing Jess critically, and when she nodded the radiographer frowned. 'I'm not too happy about that bruise on your forehead. I think we'll X-ray it as well.'

'If you're hoping to find any brains, I wouldn't hold your breath,' Ezra murmured, and Will laughed.

'Too damned right. I've been telling this girl she's an idiot for the past three years. Taking on her father's practice—'

'Look, could we just get on with this?' Jess protested, scowling across at Ezra who, to her acute annoyance, merely smiled back.

It didn't take long for Fiona to check her blood pressure and temperature, and it only took a few minutes more for Bev to process the X-rays.

'Well, the bad news is you've definitely fractured your tibia and patella,' the radiographer declared. 'The good news is they're both nice clean breaks, and I can't see any indication of internal damage.'

Jess let out the breath she hadn't even known she'd been holding. OK, so she'd broken her calf bone and kneecap, which would mean eight to ten weeks in plaster, but clean breaks meant she wouldn't have to go to the mainland. Clean breaks and no internal injuries meant she could still take care of her patients.

'My turn now.' Will beamed, leading the way out of the X-ray department into the next room. 'Time for a spot of good old reduction and plastering.'

'But…but this is an operating theatre,' Ezra declared, coming to a halt on the threshold.

'We don't have a plastering department,' the anaesthetist explained. 'Frankly, we're lucky to have a hospital at all, considering the authorities would like nothing better than to shut us down. Centralisation of resources, they call it. In my opinion—'

'Yes, dear, we all know your opinion,' his wife sighed. 'But right now Jess's leg needs attending to.'

And Ezra Dunbar badly needed some fresh air, Jess

thought as she glanced up at him and saw how white he had become. Delayed shock, her professional instincts diagnosed. OK, so he hadn't been hurt in the accident, but he *had* been involved and the knowledge of what could have happened had obviously just hit him.

'Don't you think it might be better if you waited outside?' she said gently.

He thrust his hands through his hair and she saw they were shaking. Delayed shock, indeed. And delayed shock in a very big way.

'I— Right... Fine,' he muttered. 'I'll...I'll see you later, then.'

And before she could say anything else, he was gone.

Will stared after him for a second, then chuckled as he loaded a syringe with short-acting anaesthetic. 'Well, who'd have thought it? A big, strapping chap like that coming over all queasy and not even a drop of blood in sight!'

'Not everybody's as cold-blooded as you are, Will,' Jess retorted, only to flush slightly when they all stared at her in amazement. And it was hardly surprising. What on earth was she doing, leaping to a virtual stranger's defence? And not simply a stranger but the man who had landed her here in the first place. Not that any of them knew that, of course, but... 'Look, could we just get on with getting this leg of mine aligned and plastered?' she continued vexedly. 'I don't want to be here all evening!'

Ezra didn't want to be there at all as he leant his head against the waiting-room window and tried to calm his fast-beating heart.

Hell, they must all think he was an idiot. One minute he'd been fine, and the next...

It had been the smell. He'd never realised that all operating theatres probably smelt the same, but they did, and when he'd seen the table...

'Oh, hell.'

He clenched his hands tightly together and whirled round

on his heel. Think of something else. Think of *anything* else, his mind urged, before you make an ever bigger fool of yourself than you already have done.

If only he hadn't been driving so fast. If only he'd been paying attention. But he hadn't, and now...

Restlessly he paced the waiting room. What the hell were they *doing* in there? Aligning and plastering a leg shouldn't take very long. Unless, of course, they'd found some complication.

A cold sweat broke out on his forehead and he turned quickly as a door opened behind him. Fiona. And to his relief, Jess was with her.

'She's thrown up twice, and fainted once,' the staff nurse stated, holding out a bottle of pills. 'She can take two of these for the pain, but no more than eight in twenty-four hours.'

'B-but surely you're going to keep her in?' Ezra stammered, and Fiona sighed with resignation.

'She won't stay. Maybe you can make her see sense but I doubt it.'

'Jess, of course you've got to stay!' Ezra exclaimed as Fiona walked away. 'You could be suffering from shock—'

'I'm not,' she said smoothly. 'Will's plastered my leg, and given me some painkillers, so could we, please, leave now?'

'But—'

'Could you drive me down to my practice? It's not far, but...' she gazed wryly at the crutches Fiona had given her '...I don't think I could manage it on these.'

'You want to collect something?' he murmured, still stunned by the knowledge that she'd actually discharged herself.

'Not collect, no. My surgery started half an hour ago, and I don't want to keep my patients waiting any longer than necessary.'

Ezra stared at her in disbelief, then anger flooded through him. 'Are you *crazy*?'

'I happen to believe I have a duty to my patients,' Jess replied crisply. 'Now, if you could—'

'Duty be damned!' he flared. 'You're just being pig-headed, that's all, and if you think I'm going to encourage you in this stupidity, you can think again!'

'Then I'll phone the garage and ask them to send a taxi,' she retorted, only to suddenly remember to her chagrin that, though she'd insisted on him retrieving her medical bag from her car, she'd forgotten all about her handbag. 'Could…could you lend me twenty pence for the pay-phone, please?'

'No, I will *not* lend you twenty pence!' he thundered. 'For God's sake, woman, were you born with a vacant space between your ears? You've been in a car crash. You've fractured your leg in two places, and badly bruised your forehead. OK, so maybe you don't feel too awful at the moment, but that's only because of the anaesthetic and the fact that your body's producing its own endorphins. Believe me, in a little while you're going to feel hellish—'

'Endorphins?' A frown pleated Jess's forehead. 'What do you know about endorphins?'

'Only what everybody knows,' he replied with irritation. 'That they're peptides produced in the brain which give pain-relieving effects.'

'Everybody doesn't know that,' she said, her eyes fixed on him. 'What are you—a nurse, a vet?'

'I used to be a doctor. Jess, listen to me. You can't possibly do this—'

'What kind of a doctor?'

'Does it matter?' he retorted, exasperation plain in his voice. 'The most important thing right now—'

'You can't have retired,' she continued thoughtfully. 'You're much too young to have retired.'

'I…I just don't practise any more, OK?' he muttered, his eyes not meeting hers. 'People change careers, want to do something else.'

'I can't ever imagine not wanting to be a doctor,' she

observed. 'It was something I wanted even when I was a little girl.'

'Everybody's different.'

'Yes, but—'

'Look, if you insist on going to your surgery, let's go,' he interrupted grimly. 'And I only hope to heaven that when we get there we'll find somebody who can convince you that you're out of your tiny mind!'

Tracy Maxwell tried. Ezra had to give the teenager credit for that. She might look a bit weird, with her heavily gelled, spiky black hair and the diamond stud in her nose, but the minute the receptionist saw Jess, she tried her level best.

'It's only the usual bunch of hypochondriacs anyway, Jess,' she protested. 'And you look shattered.'

'My thoughts exactly.' Ezra nodded. 'So why don't I go out to the waiting room, explain what's happened—?'

'Don't you dare!' Jess ordered. 'OK, so I've fractured my leg but my brain's still working.'

'I'd say that was highly debatable,' Ezra observed, and Tracy giggled.

'His name is Dr Dunbar,' Jess said acidly in answer to the girl's raised eyebrows. 'He has a big mouth, and even bigger opinions.'

'You're a *doctor*,' the receptionist exclaimed. 'We all thought—'

'Yes, I know what you all thought.' Ezra's lips curved ruefully. 'Sorry to be such a disappointment.'

'Oh, not a disappointment at all,' Tracy replied, batting her heavily mascara'd eyelashes at him. 'In fact, it's terrific, being able to finally put a face to a name.'

'Is it?' he said in surprise.

'Oh, yes.' Tracy beamed. 'You know, you really ought to get out more. Living all alone at Selkie Cottage—a man could start getting weird doing that, and we're quite a sociable crowd on Greensay, so there's no need for you to ever feel lonely or isolated.'

'I'm not—'

'In fact, there's a dance in the village hall this week-end—'

'Look, I'm sorry to interrupt this cosy chat,' Jess said caustically, 'but some of us have work to do. Goodbye, Dr Dunbar.' She didn't extend a hand to him but kept both fixed firmly on her crutches. 'I'd like to say it's been a pleasure meeting you, but in the circumstances I don't think that would be appropriate, do you?'

'Goodbye?' he echoed. 'But—'

'Good*bye*, Dr Dunbar,' she repeated, and before he could stop her she'd turned and hopped with as much dignity as she could along to her consulting room.

The nerve of the man—the sheer unmitigated gall! Laughing and joking with Tracy—discussing the dance which was going to be held in the village hall on Saturday. Well, to be fair, Tracy had done most of the laughing and joking, but that didn't alter the fact that *she* wouldn't be able to do any dancing for the next three months. And whose fault was that? Ezra's!

Just as it was also his fault that by the end of her surgery she felt like a washed-out rag. Ten patients—that's all she'd seen. Ten patients who'd been suffering from nothing more challenging than the usual collection of winter coughs and colds, and yet by the time they'd all gone her head was throbbing quite as badly as her leg.

So the last person she wanted to see in the waiting room was Ezra Dunbar.

'Now, before you chew my head off,' he began, getting quickly to his feet as he saw the martial glint in her eye. 'I'm here solely because I thought you might appreciate a lift home, rather than having to wait for a taxi.'

'I don't need—'

'No, I know you don't,' he interrupted. 'But just humour me this once, please, Jess, hmm?'

And because she felt so wretched she feebly allowed him

to drive her home, and made only a token protest when he insisted on helping her inside.

But the minute he'd flicked on the sitting-room light and ushered her towards a chair, she turned to him firmly. 'I'll say goodnight, then.'

To her surprise, he didn't go. Instead, he stared round the room, then back at her with a frown. 'Isn't there anybody I can call to come over and stay with you?'

'I don't need anybody,' she insisted. 'You can see for yourself that my house has no stairs, and as all I want to do is go to bed—'

'Your clothes—what about your clothes?' he demanded, his eyes taking in her green sweater and the remnants of her trousers. 'How are you going to get them off?'

'The same way I put them on,' she replied dismissively, only to see his frown increase. 'Look, I'll be all right.'

'You won't. Oh, I don't mean simply tonight,' he continued as she tried to interrupt. 'I mean tomorrow, and the day after that. Jess, you're going to be in plaster for a minimum of eight weeks. You might just be able to do your surgeries, but how are you going to do any home visits or night calls when you can't drive?'

'I'll get a locum to cover the nights and home visits.'

'And until he or she arrives, how are you planning on getting to your patients—by hopping or crawling?'

Ezra was right. If she couldn't drive there was no way she was going to be able to cope. And then suddenly it hit her. She had the answer standing right in front of her. All six feet two of him.

'You could drive me about.'

'I could *what*?' he gasped.

'You're here on holiday,' she continued quickly. 'You could drive me to my home visits and out to any night calls until I get a locum.'

'Jess—'

'I'm not asking you to do anything medical—'

'Just as well because I wouldn't do it,' he retorted. 'No, Jess. No way.'

He meant it—she could see that—but desperate situations called for desperate measures, and she drew herself up to her full five feet two inches and took a deep breath.

'OK, I've tried asking, and now I'm telling. You've admitted the accident was your fault so you owe me. Either you agree to chauffeur me around or…or I go straight to PC Inglis, and accuse you of dangerous driving.'

'That's…that's blackmail!' he spluttered, and she coloured.

'I haven't got any choice—can't you see that? The people here need me, and everybody else on the island is either too young, or too old, or they've got full-time jobs. Only you are here on holiday.'

He stared back at her impotently. He could tell her to go to hell. He could say he didn't give a damn if she spoke to the chief constable of the area himself, but if she called in the police questions would be asked. Questions about where he'd come from and what he was doing here. And everything would come out. Every last, sorry detail. There was nothing he could do but agree to her suggestion, but that didn't mean he had to like it, or that he couldn't make one last attempt to dissuade her.

'And what if I am a drug dealer, like Wattie Hope said, or an axe murderer?'

Heavens, but he looked angry enough at the moment to be either, she thought as she stared up at him. And she couldn't really blame him. What she was doing was unforgivable.

'I'll…I'll risk it,' she said. He didn't reply. He simply turned on his heel and headed for her front door, and desperately she hopped after him. 'Look, I'm sorry. I know what I'm doing is wrong, and I promise I'll phone the agency about a locum first thing tomorrow—'

She was talking to thin air, and as she listened to the sound of his footsteps going down the gravel path she suddenly felt an overwhelming desire to burst into tears. Which was crazy.

Dammit, he owed her a favour. OK, so maybe she shouldn't have blackmailed him into agreeing to it, but he *did* owe her. And just because he obviously thought she was the lowest form of pond life, that was no reason for her to get upset.

She was home, wasn't she? Home in the house where she'd been born. Home with all her familiar things. OK, so her leg—not to mention every other bone in her body— hurt like hell, but that didn't explain why she should suddenly feel so lost and lonely.

And it sure as heck didn't explain why her heart should lift when her front door was suddenly thrown open again and Ezra reappeared.

'I can't do it,' he announced without preamble. 'You might be the most manipulative, stubbornly vexatious woman it's ever been my misfortune to meet, but I can't leave you here on your own. You could collapse in the middle of the night—'

'I won't—and if I do it's not your problem,' she pointed out.

'Of course it's my problem,' he flared. 'You wouldn't be in this mess if it wasn't for me, and if you're too stupid and pigheaded to stay in hospital there's only one thing I can do. I'll have to stay.'

'Stay?' she echoed faintly.

'And not just for tonight,' he fumed. 'If you insist on me being at your beck and call twenty-four hours a day I'm going to have to move in with you until you get a locum.'

Jess's mouth opened and closed soundlessly, then she found her voice. 'But it could take me a week to organise a locum!'

His lip curled grimly. 'You're the blackmailer. You tell me what other alternative there is?'

To her acute dismay Jess realised there wasn't one. His cottage was on the far west side of the island and if she got an emergency call during the night he'd have to get up, get dressed, drive down, pick her up—

'And lose vital, potentially life-threatening minutes in the process.' Ezra nodded, obviously reading her mind. 'So would you care to reconsider your plan?'

She wanted to—oh, boy, did she want to. But she couldn't. She couldn't abandon her patients, leaving them with no emergency cover or home visits.

'No, I don't want to reconsider,' she replied tightly. 'Believe me, the thought of you living here doesn't exactly fill me with unmitigated joy either, but right now it looks as though I'm stuck with you, Dr Dunbar.'

And she was stuck with him, she thought after she'd shown him through to the spare room then retreated thankfully to her own bedroom. Stuck with the most bossy, self-opinionated man she'd ever had the misfortune to meet. Stuck with a complete stranger who could have been anyone, despite his declaration that he'd once been a doctor.

Yet, as she began undressing, and heard him moving about in the room next to hers, she realised that she had that odd feeling of security again.

And she was still mad.

CHAPTER TWO

IT WAS the sunlight streaming through her bedroom window which first told Jess something was wrong.

For a start it should be dark. Greensay was situated off
the far west coast of Scotland and it never became fully
light in January until well after nine o'clock, so if the sun
was shining…

Quickly she reached for her bedside clock, remembered
her plastered leg too late, and with a yelp of pain knocked
the clock. But not before she'd seen the time. One o'clock.
Lunchtime. Which could only mean some officious, overbearing swine had sneaked into her room during the night
and switched off her alarm.

The same overbearing, officious swine whose dark head
had just appeared round her bedroom door.

'Now, before you blow a fuse,' Ezra declared, holding
up his hands defensively as she eased herself upright, a look
of fury plain upon her face, 'it was obvious you needed
sleep—'

'And what about my morning surgery?' she exclaimed,
pushing her tangled hair back out of her eyes and wincing
as her fingers caught the bruise on her forehead. 'My poor
patients, left wondering where I was—'

'They weren't. I told Tracy to put a notice on the health-
centre door, explaining what had happened and advising
anyone with worrying symptoms to contact the Sinclair
Memorial.'

She all but ground her teeth. 'Dr Dunbar—'

'The name's Ezra.'

'Tracy doesn't have the authority to cancel anything. She

only joined my practice four months ago. Cath Stewart's my senior receptionist and practice nurse.'

'I wondered about that,' he observed. 'The diamond stud in her nose and everything.'

'There's nothing wrong with the stud,' she retorted, conveniently forgetting her own initial misgivings when she'd seen it. 'It's fashionable, modern. And how Tracy dresses is none of your damn business anyway,' she added for good measure.

He stared at her for a second, then sighed heavily. 'Topsy.'

'I beg your pardon?'

'Forget it. Jess, a tired doctor is a careless doctor. A tired doctor who is also in pain is a menace.'

'I'm not in pain,' she lied.

His eyebrows rose. 'No? Then lunch will be ready in ten minutes. No doubt you'll be able to get up, dressed and along to the kitchen by then.'

And he went. Without giving her the chance to hurl something harder than her voice at him, he just upped and went.

Of all the interfering, arrogant, pompous...! There was no limit to the home truths she intended throwing at him, but first she had to get out of bed and dressed.

Well, she'd managed to get undressed and into bed last night, she told herself as she pulled back the duvet and stared dubiously at her plastered leg. How hard could it be to do it in reverse?

Tear-blindingly, excruciatingly hard was the answer.

'Don't say a word,' she ordered when she finally made it to the kitchen more than half an hour later. 'Not one single solitary one, OK?'

Obediently Ezra lifted the pan of potatoes off the hob and drained them. 'It's frozen fish, potatoes and peas for lunch. Your freezer needs restocking.'

She knew it did. In fact, she'd intended going shopping yesterday but it hardly seemed tactful to point out to him why she hadn't been able to do it. Especially when he was cooking for her.

'Who—or what—is Topsy?' she said instead when he put her lunch down in front of her.

'A neighbour's cat in London.'

Which made absolutely no sense at all to her, Ezra realised as he began washing the pots, but perfect sense to him.

Topsy and Jess Arden had a lot in common. Both were red-haired, green-eyed and fiercely independent. Both hissed and spat fire whenever they thought anyone was trying to invade their space. Not that he'd tried invading Topsy's space often. He preferred his hands in one piece. And he most certainly didn't intend trying it with Jess Arden.

Lord, but she was a firebrand and a half. Attractive, he supposed, if your taste ran to shoulder-length, curly red hair and eyes which sparkled like emeralds. Sassy and spunky too, but he'd never been attracted to redheads, and certainly not to redheads who were stubborn, opinionated and pigheaded. And Jess Arden was one pigheaded lady.

'OK, I'm ready to go.'

He turned in surprise and gave her suspiciously clean plate a very hard stare. 'Go where?'

'I may have missed my morning surgery, but I have absolutely no intention of missing any home visits or my evening surgery.'

Ezra reached for a towel to dry his hands. 'I don't suppose there's any point in me trying to talk you out of it, is there? No, I didn't think there was,' he sighed when she pointedly lifted her medical bag. 'Have you taken your painkillers?'

'Of course,' she replied quickly. Much too quickly, he thought, but before he could press her she continued, 'So, are we going, or what?'

He would have preferred the 'or what' if it meant her returning to bed and staying there, but he also knew that nothing short of a padlock and chain would have kept Jess Arden in her bed.

Actually, the image held a certain appeal, he decided grimly as he followed her out of the house. Especially if he could have arranged to have her fed on nothing but bread and water for a couple of weeks. Perhaps that would teach her the perils of blackmailing someone, and it might even—though he very much doubted it—teach her some sense.

'I'll have to leave you at your surgery for a little while,' he declared after he'd helped her into his car. 'I'm not sure how long I'll be—'

'But you agreed to chauffeur me about,' Jess protested. 'We had a deal—'

'Which I fully intend to keep,' he interrupted, his voice clipped, 'but unless you want me arrested for driving an unroadworthy vehicle, I suggest I get my car repaired first.'

She bit her lip. 'Oh. I see. I'm sorry,' she added belatedly.

He didn't reply. In fact, he didn't say anything at all during the drive down to Inverlairg, which left her feeling angry, and guilty, and confused, all at the same time.

The trouble was, she wasn't used to being fussed over. She was used to making her own decisions, and although part of her knew her leg wouldn't have been broken if it hadn't been for him, the other part also knew he hadn't needed to make her lunch or to switch off her alarm to let her get some sleep. And how had she repaid him? By sounding like a nagging harpy, that was how.

She would just have to apologise to him again properly, she decided when he left her outside the health centre and drove away without a backward glance. And then again perhaps she wouldn't, she thought when she saw the notice taped to the door, proclaiming that all medical services were suspended until further notice.

'I'm sure Dr Dunbar meant it for the best, Jess,' Cath declared when she bore the offending notice into the surgery. 'He probably thought—as we all did—that you'd be taking a few days off.'

'Well, you all thought wrong,' Jess replied as evenly as she could. 'Dr Dunbar and I have had a full and frank discussion.' Well, that was one way of putting it, she thought, remembering her threat of police action. 'And he has kindly volunteered to chauffeur me around until I can get a locum, so it's business as usual, starting with my home visits this afternoon and evening surgery tonight.'

'But what about your night calls?' the receptionist protested. 'I can do some for you—after ten years as a theatre sister at the Sinclair Memorial I've certainly got the experience—but there's a limit to what I'd feel happy about treating on my own.'

To her acute annoyance Jess felt her cheeks beginning to heat up. 'Dr Dunbar has also volunteered to stay at my cottage so he can drive me to any night-time emergencies.'

Cath's eyes opened very wide, then a slow grin spread across her face. 'I can just imagine what Wattie Hope is going to make of *that* arrangement!'

'Cath—'

'Tracy said he reminded her of a pirate. All dark and bearded and mysterious.'

'Personally, I've always thought men with beards have something to hide,' Jess declared dampeningly.

'Tracy also said he wasn't wearing a wedding ring. So do you reckon he's single, married or divorced?'

'I've no idea, and less interest,' Jess replied dismissively. 'And I thought Tracy was dating Danny Hislop anyway?' she added with irritation, only to be angry with herself for *being* irritated.

'She is,' Cath observed, shooting her a puzzled glance. 'But she's known him since they were kids, whereas Ezra… Well, he's new, different.'

Oh, he was different, all right. Bossy, opinionated—a human steamroller. And yet he could also be very kind,

Jess was forced to admit when she suddenly remembered
what was inside her medical bag.

Gingerly she delved into it and extracted a soggy pack-
age. 'Cath, could you get rid of this for me, please?'

Her receptionist wrinkled her nose. 'It smells like fish.'

'Fish, potatoes and peas, to be exact. Dr Dunbar made
me lunch, but I felt too queasy to eat it.'

'And you *hid* it?' Cath laughed. 'Boy, this must be some
man if you didn't want to risk offending him!'

'It wasn't that—well, it was in a way—but I didn't—I
mean, I wasn't...' Cath's brown eyes were dancing, and
Jess scowled. 'Look, could you just get rid of it, please,
while I phone the medical agency about a locum?'

But by the time Jess had finished speaking to the agency
she heartily wished that someone—or something—could
have got rid of Ezra Dunbar before he'd ever set foot on
Greensay. Oh, the agency was very nice, very sympathetic,
but the minute she'd told them where her practice was, the
excuses had begun. January was a difficult month for lo-
cums, trainees didn't like being sent to remote areas, it was
all rather short notice. After fifteen minutes of begging and
pleading, the best she could extract from them was the
promise of a locum in five weeks.

'If Dr Dunbar's as wonderful as Tracy says, I'd just sit
back and enjoy it,' Cath replied when Jess told her. 'After
all, it's not every day a handsome pirate comes to the res-
cue of a damsel in distress, takes her home and then cooks
for her!'

And it wasn't every day that Jess saw her happily married forty-year-old receptionist light up like a beacon, but
she did just that when the door to the health centre opened
and Ezra appeared.

Good grief, anyone would think he was a film star, Jess
thought with disgust. OK, so he was six feet two inches
tall, with thick black hair, and had rather nice grey eyes
when he smiled. And, OK, his voice was deep and warm,
and oddly comforting when he wasn't shouting at you, but

when all was said and done he was just a man. And yet now, not only had Tracy gone all dreamy-eyed over him, Cath clearly thought he was Mr Wonderful, too.

Irritably she picked up the list detailing requests for home visits and frowned when she scanned it. 'Mairi Morrison wants a home visit?'

'Actually, it was her neighbour, Grace Henderson, who asked if you could drop by,' Cath replied. 'Apparently she's a bit worried about her.'

Jess's frown deepened. Grace must be worried if she was prepared to risk incurring Mairi's wrath by asking for a home visit on her behalf. There wasn't a person on Greensay who didn't know that Mairi never asked for or expected help from anyone.

'Something wrong?' Ezra asked as she grasped her crutches.

'Maybe—I don't know,' she replied absently, then pulled herself together. 'My first call is to Harbour Road. Toby Ralston—four years old—juvenile arthritis. His parents initially thought he had meningitis. I confess I did, too, when they called me out in the middle of the night and I discovered his temperature was over 39°C, and he had stiffness in his joints and a rash.'

'Systemic juvenile arthritis, then, affecting the small joints rather than pauciarticular or polyarticular arthritis?' he said, then smiled slightly as she stared at him in surprise. 'I did tell you I used to be a doctor, remember?'

He had, and she'd believed him—of course she had—but she'd have been a fool if a little part of her hadn't wondered about his qualifications. She wasn't wondering any more.

'I've got him on non-steroidal anti-inflammatory drugs to relieve the pain and swelling, but they're not working very well,' she continued once Ezra had stowed her medical bag in the boot of his car and they were driving down the narrow streets from the health centre towards the white-washed houses that lined the harbour. 'I suppose I could start him on corticosteroids but...'

'You're reluctant to do so because of his age.' Ezra nodded. 'I'd try to keep it under control for the moment. Most children recover from juvenile arthritis within a few years and are left with little or no disability. Only a very small minority go on to develop an adult form of arthritis.'

She'd been telling Toby's parents that for weeks, but the minute Simon and Elspeth had heard the word 'arthritis' they'd instantly assumed their son would be crippled for life, and nothing she'd said had persuaded them otherwise. Which was why, when Ezra drew his car to a halt outside the Ralstons' home, she found herself turning to him and saying on impulse, 'Would you like to come in—see him yourself?'

'I'm not a doctor any more.'

'I know, but I wondered—'

'*No!*' He bit his lip as she stared up at him, startled by his vehemence. 'No,' he repeated more evenly. 'I'll wait outside in the car if you don't mind.'

Jess didn't mind at all. It wasn't as though she didn't know what was wrong with Toby, but what really intrigued her was why Ezra had reacted as he had. OK, so he didn't practise medicine any more but he'd seemed not only angered by her suggestion but also strangely upset by it.

It didn't make any sense, but she had no time to think about it. Elspeth was already on the doorstep and Toby was bouncing towards her, his white-blond hair gleaming in the sunlight, his large blue eyes alert and full of mischief.

'It's his chest, Doctor,' Elspeth explained, ushering her son back into the sitting room, concern plain on her face. 'He got up this morning with the most dreadful cold, and I know we have to be careful, what with his condition and everything.'

Jess would have been amazed if Toby's abundantly runny nose had meant anything other than one of the many colds which were plaguing the islanders this winter, and a quick check with her stethoscope revealed she was right.

'You don't think he needs a chest X-ray, then?' Elspeth said after Jess had given her the good news. 'Or perhaps some antibiotics?'

'Elspeth, he has a cold,' Jess said firmly. 'If I give him antibiotics every time he's snuffly, they won't work when he really needs them. How's the physiotherapy going?' she continued, determinedly changing the subject.

'All right, I guess. He's not very happy about the night splints.'

Which meant he probably wasn't wearing them, Jess thought with a deep sigh. 'Elspeth, you know he has to wear them in bed, whether he wants to or not. The physiotherapy he's getting will maintain muscle strength and joint mobility, but the splints are equally important to prevent joint deformity.'

'I suppose so,' the woman muttered. 'I still don't know how he's got this juvenile arthritis. Simon's phoned round all our relatives—even contacted his uncle in Australia—but none of them can remember anybody in the family ever having had it.'

'Elspeth, I only said it *might* be inherited,' Jess reminded her. 'The initial joint inflammation can also be triggered by a viral infection, but the truth is we really don't know why some children are affected and others aren't. But as I told you before, there's every chance he'll grow out of it.'

And Elspeth still didn't believe her, Jess thought wearily when she left the house and Ezra drove her to her next call. Neither did Denise Fullarton after she'd examined her, but at least the local dentist's wife had more cause to be concerned.

'She's had three miscarriages in five years?' Ezra exclaimed when she explained the situation. 'No wonder she was too terrified to walk to the surgery for a confirmation of her pregnancy. How far on is she?'

'Seven weeks.'

'Has she ever carried a baby to full term?'

Jess shook her head. 'I've had her tested for everything—fibroids, uterine abnormality, genetic abnormalities—but the muscles of her cervix just seem to be too weak to support her uterus when she's pregnant. I've told her I'll put a stitch in her cervix to keep it closed when she reaches the end of her first trimester, but the trouble is she doesn't usually make it to twelve weeks.'

'Have you tried taking blood tests at the start of her menstrual cycle to see whether her progesterone levels are raised?' Ezra suggested. 'I believe there's some evidence to suggest women who miscarry a lot don't produce enough progesterone after ovulation to help the embryo.'

She looked up at him enquiringly. 'I thought that was usually linked to polycystic ovarian disease?'

'It is,' he said nodding, 'but I also remember reading that giving gonadotrophin-releasing hormones to women who repeatedly miscarry can help. It's obviously too late to try that now, but if—and hopefully it doesn't happen again—your patient has another miscarriage it might be worth a try.'

It would, just as she'd dearly have liked to have asked him what kind of doctor he'd been before he'd decided to stop practising medicine.

Not a GP, that was for sure. This was a man who was used to giving orders—orders that were instantly obeyed.

A special registrar, perhaps? But, then, why had he given it up? He didn't look like the kind of man who would throw in the towel on a whim. Dedicated, she would have said. Focused.

Could she ask him—did she dare?

Awkwardly she cleared her throat, but before she could say anything someone called her name and she turned to see Louise Lawrence striding determinedly across the road towards her, her youngest daughter in tow.

'I wish you'd take a quick look at Sophy's head, Doctor,'

Louise said irritably. 'Scratch, scratch, scratch. She's been doing it for a couple of days now and it's driving me mad.'

Obediently Jess parted Sophy's long black hair and saw the cause immediately. 'I'm afraid your daughter has lice, Mrs Lawrence—head lice.'

Sophy's mother was outraged. 'But she can't have! My daughter has clean hair—'

'Which is just the sort lice prefer,' Jess interrupted gently. 'They generally travel from head to head when children share combs or hats—'

'But Sophy never does that,' Louise protested. 'I've warned her time and time again about the dangers, and I can assure you she doesn't do it.'

Sophy's swiftly averted gaze suggested that the warning had gone unheeded, but Jess saw no point in commenting on it. The most important thing now was to treat the condition.

'Do people often do that—ask you for a consultation on the street?' Ezra asked, clearly bemused, as an obviously furious Mrs Lawrence bore Sophy off in the direction of the village shop with instructions to buy a special head-lice shampoo and to remember to treat everybody in the family.

'And how!' Jess chuckled. 'My most potentially embarrassing case happened not long after I came back to the island. It was an old fisherman who thought he had a hernia but didn't want to take time off work to come into the surgery to confirm it. Honestly, if anyone had seen the two of us down this side street—me on my knees in front of him—well, you can just imagine what they would have thought!'

Unfortunately Ezra discovered he could—only too vividly—and was even more dismayed to feel his groin tighten at the image.

Lord, but Tracy had been right. One week of living on his own at Selkie Cottage and already he was getting weird. He had to be if he was finding himself envying an unknown, elderly fisherman with a hernia.

And the ridiculous thing was that he didn't even *like* Jess Arden. OK, so in the winter sunshine her red hair shone like spun silk, and her eyes became an even deeper green than they'd been before, but when all was said and done she was just a woman.

And a blackmailing one at that, he reminded himself as he drove her out of Inverlairg to the first of her outlying home visits.

So if she wanted to hobble from patient to patient all afternoon, he had absolutely no sympathy for her. And if she was clearly growing more and more exhausted by the minute, then it was her own fault.

Which was why it made no sense at all when he drew his car to a halt outside Woodside croft for him to demand angrily, 'Look, how many more of these damn house calls have you got to make?'

Of course she bristled immediately, as any idiot would have known she would.

'I'm sorry if you're bored, Dr Dunbar,' she said, her voice ice-cold, 'but I'm not about to rush my visits just to please you.'

'I'm not bored—'

'This is my last call,' she continued, completely ignoring his protest, 'but, believe me, it will take as long as it takes.'

And it would, she thought, even though she was obviously the last person Mairi Morrison wanted to see when she opened her front door.

'Not much of a talker, your new locum,' Mairi observed when Ezra stalked off towards the barns after the very briefest of greetings.

'People on the mainland don't tend to talk as much as we do, Mairi, and I'm afraid I might have rather steam-rollered him a bit today, and...' And what the hell was she doing, defending him? Jess wondered, feeling her cheeks redden under Mairi's curious gaze. Ezra Dunbar was big enough and cussed enough to look after himself. 'Grace asked me to drop by,' she continued quickly. 'She's a bit worried about you.'

Mairi shook her head as she led the way into the house. 'I'd have thought she had enough to worry about with her own angina, instead of poking her nose into other people's business. I'm just getting old, like everybody else.'

'Fifty-three's hardly old,' Jess protested with a laugh. 'In fact, I'd say you were just in your prime!'

The Mairi Morrison Jess knew of old would have made some witty retort. The same Mairi Morrison would also have had something considerably more stringent to say about interfering neighbours, but this Mairi Morrison accepted her offer of an examination without a murmur and to Jess's dismay seemed lethargic and uninterested, almost strangely resigned.

'How long have you had that cough?' Jess asked after she'd sounded her.

'Everybody's got a cold, Jess. It's winter.'

It was, but everybody's chest didn't sound like Mairi's. Thick and congested and wheezy. And everybody hadn't lost weight they could ill afford to lose.

'I'd like to send you for an X-ray,' she said, reaching for her notebook. 'You've probably simply got a chest infection, but it's best to check it out. I'll give Bev a call and try to get you an appointment for the end of the week, if that's OK?'

Mairi gazed down at her red, work-worn knuckles for a moment, then sighed. 'I suppose so.'

There it was again. The same air of defeat, as though Mairi knew—or suspected—something she wasn't telling her.

'Mairi, if there's something worrying you—'

'When are you going to get married?'

Mairi had been asking the same question ever since Jess had turned twenty-two, but today Jess knew it was merely a means of changing the subject. She also sensed, however, that there was no point in pressing the matter, and she smiled. 'Oh, this year, next year, some time, never.'

'You've not met the man with the black hair and the cleft chin, then?' Mairi observed, and Jess stared at her in amused amazement.

'Good grief, fancy you remembering that! I must have been—what—fifteen, sixteen, when I told you all about my ideal man. No, I haven't met him yet.'

Neither had she ever experienced that flip of her heart which she'd solemnly assured Mairi would indicate she'd fallen in love with The One.

Well, actually, yes, she had, she suddenly remembered, suppressing a chuckle. Last night, when Ezra had come back, her heart had lifted in a most disconcerting way. Which only served to show what romantic twaddle she'd believed when she'd been sixteen.

'Maybe it's time you looked closer to home,' the older woman said, leading the way outside. 'Brian Guthrie's sweet on you, you know.'

'Brian's lonely, and has been ever since Leanne died.'

'He thinks you're sweet on him.'

He did, too, Jess thought glumly. She'd only gone out with him because he'd been so depressed after his wife had died, and she'd thought it might help if he had someone to talk to. And it had, but not the way she'd wanted.

'OK, so he's in his fifties,' Mairi continued, 'but at thirty-two you're no spring chicken.'

'Gee, thanks!' Jess protested, her eyes dancing as Ezra walked towards them, ready to carry her medical bag.

'And if you don't fancy Brian Guthrie, there's always Fraser Kennedy,' the older woman continued. 'He's been in love with you for years, and he owns three fishing boats now so he's well on the way to becoming a man of means.'

Jess shook her head and laughed, but she didn't feel much like laughing when Ezra drove her back to Inverlairg and she saw how full her evening surgery was. She felt even less like laughing by the time she'd finished it.

'Time to go home, Jess,' Ezra declared firmly when she came out of her consulting room, and he saw the dark shadows under her eyes, the way she was leaning more heavily on her crutches.

For once she didn't argue. All she wanted was to go home and crawl into bed, but even when they reached her cottage he was still in full organising mode.

'Put your feet up, and I'll get dinner,' he said, steering her into the sitting room. 'It's nothing fancy—just some chicken I picked up from the shop—but I'll make a proper list tomorrow—'

'I'd rather just skip dinner tonight if you don't mind,' she said swiftly, only to see his eyebrows snap down. 'Look, missing one meal isn't going to do me any harm. It's not as though I'm fading away—far from it—and I had a good lunch—'

'So how come I smelt fish every time I lifted your medical bag?'

A tide of bright colour swept across her cheeks. She'd hoped he hadn't noticed, but he clearly had, and she doubted whether he'd believe her if she said he'd simply been smelling Greensay's fresh sea breezes.

'I...I didn't want to offend you when you'd obviously gone to so much trouble—'

'You don't like my cooking?'

'No—I mean, yes, it was fine, great,' she floundered. 'I just felt a little queasy at lunchtime. Probably a side effect from the anaesthetic Will gave me last night.'

His eyes narrowed, and she could almost see his professional instincts working as he stared at the bruise on her forehead. 'And do you feel sick now—headachy, dizzy?'

'I'm just tired, that's all.'

'Then you'll eat,' he said firmly.

And she did, though he very much doubted whether she knew what she was eating.

Hell, but she looked awful. Half-asleep on her feet, her

face chalk white with fatigue and pain. She couldn't go on like this, and somehow he had to make her see it.

'Jess.'

He'd spoken softly but her eyes flew open at once. 'I'm not asleep. Just resting my eyes.'

'Resting them, be damned. Jess, this arrangement we've got—it isn't working.'

'Of course it's working,' she exclaimed, panic plain on her face. 'OK, so maybe we need to iron out one or two creases—'

'You're going to kill yourself if you go on like this,' he said bluntly. 'You're not taking your painkillers—'

'I am!' she protested. 'Just because you haven't seen me—'

'Jess, I know exactly how many you've taken,' he interrupted, pulling her bottle of pills out of his pocket and waving them under her nose. 'Two, that's all, and you took those last night.'

She bit her lip. 'I can't take too many—you know I can't. They fuddle your brains, make you sleepy.'

'Jess—'

'I know what you're going to say—that I should close the surgery until I can get a locum—but the agency can't get me anyone for five weeks—'

'Five *weeks*!' he repeated in horror, and she groaned inwardly.

She'd meant to break the news to him gently, not spring it on him like this, but it was too late now.

'It's an awful lot longer than I expected, too,' she said, 'but I can't—and won't—ask my patients to travel to the mainland, so I have to keep on working—can't you see that?'

He could, and the trouble was he could also see an obvious solution to her problem, but it was a solution he didn't want to suggest. A year ago he'd vowed never to set foot in any medical establishment again unless he was a patient. Hell, that was why he'd come to Greensay, for anonymity, and yet…

Look at her, his mind urged. Hell, the girl's in pain. It's your fault, and if you can do even a little to help, you have to.

He cleared his throat, knowing he was undoubtedly going to regret what he was about to say, but seeing no other alternative.

'Jess, I can't offer to do your home visits and night calls—I wouldn't feel comfortable, not knowing any of your patients' medical histories—but would it help if I shared your surgeries until your locum arrives?'

She stared at him in amazement. Would it help? It was an offer to die for.

'I—I don't know what to say,' she stammered.

'How about "Yes, please, Ezra" and "Thank you?"' he replied, forcing a smile to his lips.

'Yes, for sure, but a mere thank you…' She shook her head. 'Ezra, I know this isn't how you planned on spending your holiday. You probably came here to paint, or to write, or something.' She paused, giving him the chance to explain, but he didn't. 'I guess what I'm trying to say is how very grateful I am, and…' To her dismay tears filled her eyes and she blinked them away quickly. 'I'll be forever in your debt.'

Ezra groaned inwardly as he saw the tears. Jess was a spunky, stroppy, irritating lady, and the last thing he wanted was to see she could be vulnerable, too.

Vulnerable meant him noticing how soft and husky her voice became when she was deeply moved. Vulnerable meant him seeing the way her green eyes darkened, throwing the whiteness and translucency of her skin into sharp relief. And he didn't want to see these things. Seeing them meant he was in danger of forgetting why he was here, and that the last thing he needed in his life was a relationship.

'You ought to be in bed,' he said gruffly. 'You're almost asleep on your feet.'

'Does this mean you'll be moving back to your own cottage?'

His heart lifted at the prospect, only to plummet down again as he thought it through. 'I can't. You're obviously not fit enough yet to be left on your own. No, don't try to argue with me, Jess,' he continued as she opened her mouth to do just that. 'If I say you're not fit, you're not fit. Just accept that you're stuck with me for a little while longer.'

And he was stuck, too, he realised when she smiled up at him—a small, wobbly smile which touched him more than he could say. Stuck with a job he didn't want, in the company of a girl who somehow seemed to be unaccountably growing more and more attractive by the hour.

He groaned inwardly again.

CHAPTER THREE

'I'M so glad it's you, Dr Arden,' Wattie Hope said, sitting down opposite her with an ingratiating smile. 'This new chap you've got—nice enough bloke and everything, but you go in to see him with an ingrowing toenail and before you know it he's got you stripped, sounded and your blood pressure taken.'

'And how is the ingrowing toenail?' Jess asked evenly as she opened his file.

'Och, 'twas just an expression, Doctor,' Wattie replied, his smile widening to reveal a row of tobacco-stained teeth. 'It's the old trouble—my back, you know.'

Jess did know, just as she also knew that Wattie's back seemed to possess a marked tendency to get worse whenever work was mentioned, then miraculously improve the minute he heard someone was buying drinks in the local pub.

'Have you found the pills Dr Dunbar prescribed helpful?' she asked, scanning Ezra's notes. 'I see he's started you on a course of indomethacin—'

'They helped a wee bit, but...' Wattie heaved a sigh. 'Not as much as I'd hoped.'

Probably because you're not taking them, you old fraud, Jess thought grimly. 'It might be worth increasing the dose—'

'Ronald at the garage told me you were speeding when you crashed into Dr Dunbar's car.' Wattie shook his head in wonder. 'And there was me thinking you were one of the most careful drivers on the island, Doctor.'

PC Inglis had said the same, Jess remembered, when she'd reported her wrecked car. His sharply raised eyebrows had also told her he wasn't one bit deceived by her story, but if that was the way she wanted to play it, so be it.

'Wattie—'

'Dr Dunbar was a doctor in London, so I understand,' he continued. 'Now, would he have been an ordinary GP there, or one of those big-shot Harley Street doctors?'

'I think you'd better ask Dr Dunbar that yourself,' Jess replied. With any luck he would, and with a little bit of extra luck she might be there when Ezra sent him away with a flea in his ear. 'Now, about these pills—'

'Wasn't it a stroke of luck he turned out to be a doctor? I mean, if it had been anybody else...' Wattie shook his head. 'Where would we all have been?'

'Yes—quite,' Jess said tightly. 'Now, as I was saying—'

'And lucky, too, that your father's old house has two bedrooms in it, now that Dr Dunbar's staying with you. It does have two bedrooms, doesn't it?'

Didn't Wattie ever give up? Apparently not, judging by the way his small, dark eyes were surveying her speculatively, like a crow contemplating a worm. Well, she'd had quite enough, she decided, snapping his folder shut.

'As you've only been taking the indomethacin for a week, I think we'll give it a little longer to see if it will help,' she declared, reaching for her crutches. 'If you still don't find any improvement in a fortnight, come back and we'll try something else.'

That Wattie did not take kindly to this abrupt conclusion to his consultation was plain. He got to his feet, rammed his cloth cap back on his head and fixed her with a baleful glare.

'Just as long as it's you I see, Doctor. Some of us have got better things to do than be turned inside out by a man who would make the rocks on the seashore look talkative.'

Anger surged within her as she accompanied him back to the waiting room, but much as she longed to deny his criticisms she knew she couldn't. Ezra *did* take a long time examining his patients, and it wasn't because he was chatting to them.

'Doesn't say much, your new chap,' her regulars had commented. 'In fact, he can be a bit brusque at times but, my word, is he thorough.'

So thorough that the number of blood samples they'd been sending off to the mainland had doubled since he'd joined the practice a week ago. So thorough that Bev Grant had jokingly said she'd soon be a full-time radiographer instead of a part-time one.

If it had been anyone else Jess would have wondered if Ezra's thoroughness masked a massive case of insecurity, but he was the least insecure man she'd ever met.

'Wattie doesn't look very happy,' Cath observed as he strode out of the surgery, frustration on his face.

'Wattie Hope is a pain in the butt,' Jess replied. She glanced out at the waiting room. It was empty, apart from Miss Tweedie. 'Has Robb MacGregor cancelled his twelve o'clock appointment with me?'

'Not as far as I know,' Cath replied, reaching to answer the phone. 'Good morning. Inverlairg Health Centre. Oh, hello, Fraser.' Quickly, she transferred the telephone receiver to her other ear and picked up a pencil. 'I can give you an appointment with Dr Arden— Oh, you'd rather see Dr Dunbar? It would have to be Monday, then. OK, we'll see you Monday at 9.30.'

'Looks like you've got yourself a fan.' Jess smiled, seeing Ezra come out of his consulting room.

He didn't look particularly thrilled by the information. In fact, he looked downright puzzled.

'Jess, what do you know about gout?'

'Gout?' she repeated in surprise as the surgery phone rang again. 'Not a lot, except it was previously thought to be caused by too much rich food and alcohol, but we now know it occurs when the kidneys aren't excreting enough uric acid.' She ran her finger along the selection of medical books they kept in the office and pulled one out. 'Who do you think has—?'

'Sorry, Jess, but it's Virginia—the Dawson's Pharmaceuticals rep,' Cath declared, cradling the telephone against her chest. 'She wants to know if you've had a chance to look through her catalogue yet?' Jess drew a finger across her throat expressively, and Cath smothered a chuckle as she put the phone back to her ear. 'So sorry, Miss Brunton, but Dr Arden's decided not to buy anything this time. Yes, I'll be sure to tell her you called.'

'That woman is driving me nuts,' Jess groaned when Cath replaced the receiver. 'One order—that's all I've ever given her—and now she haunts me.'

'Told you it was a mistake, didn't I?' the receptionist said. 'Give these reps an inch, and they'll take a mile.'

Tracy could have done with quite a few more inches, Jess thought, blinking slightly, as the girl joined them wearing a skirt that could have doubled for a pelmet.

'We've plenty of the MMR vaccine, but we're getting low on the diphtheria, pertussis and tetanus triple vaccine,' she declared, beaming up at Ezra as she passed him.

'Um, right. I'll order some more,' Jess replied, involuntarily glancing down at her own very sensible, calf-length skirt, before suddenly remembering Ezra's patient. 'Who do you think has—?'

She was too late. He had already disappeared back into his room.

Tracy sighed as she gazed after him. 'He's lovely, isn't he?'

Cath nodded in agreement and Jess stared at the two women in bemused disbelief. *Lovely?* For sure, Ezra could be very kind. Indeed, his offer to help with her practice had been downright amazing, but lovely as in drop-dead gorgeous? She must need her eyes tested because she sure as heck couldn't see it.

'Sorry to be so late, Doctor,' Robb MacGregor said, coming through the health centre door at a rush, 'but I've been waiting on an order from the mainland and it's finally arrived, and it's wrong. Heaven knows how it can be. Twelve tons of bricks is twelve bloody tons of bricks in anybody's language!'

And Miss Tweedie, for one, clearly didn't appreciate his, judging from the way she pointedly slammed her magazine down in the waiting room.

'Would you like to come through to my consulting room, Robb?' Jess suggested, and the builder bit his lip as he followed her.

'I'm sorry, Doctor, but if it's not one damn thing at the moment, it's another. Perhaps if I had more energy I'd be able to cope, but...' He shook his head unhappily. 'I'm so tired all the time, you see—that's one of the reasons I've come to see you—and as for being short-tempered...!'

'Are you having trouble sleeping?' Jess asked, propping her crutches by the side of her desk and sitting down.

Robb thrust a large hand through his already tousled brown hair and smiled ruefully. 'Doctor, if you were a self-employed man with a wife and two kids to support, and idiots on the mainland kept sending you the wrong goods, would *you* be sleeping?'

She chuckled. 'I guess not. Could you slip your shirt off for me?'

He did, but after Jess had given him a thorough check-up she was no wiser.

'You've lost weight since your last physical, haven't you?' she asked when Robb had put his shirt back on.

'Still need to lose a bit more, I reckon,' he replied, patting his stomach ruefully.

'Any diarrhoea or stomach pains?'

He shook his head, and she leant back in her seat with a frown. He looked at the end of his tether. He also looked tired and pale and drawn, but his heart rate had been normal, his BP the same, and apart from his stomach being a little distended she could find nothing to suggest anything worrying.

'I've taken a blood sample, and started him on a course of iron tablets in case he's slightly anaemic,' she told Ezra when he joined her in her consulting room for coffee at the end of morning surgery, 'but I keep wondering if I've missed something.'

'If he'd been suffering from stomach pain or diarrhoea I'd have said possible stomach ulcer,' Ezra said, handing her one of the cups of coffee Cath had brought in. 'But without that it certainly looks like anaemia to me.'

She wished she was more convinced, and then she remembered something else she still didn't know the answer to. 'Which of my patients did you think had gout?'

'Brian Guthrie.'

'Oh, the poor man,' she exclaimed with concern. 'Are you sure?'

'He has all the classic symptoms. A swollen toe, which is very red and tender to the touch, and the veins on the rest of his foot were quite extensively enlarged, too.'

She shook her head. 'Brian's had a really rough time lately. His wife died two years ago, and he misses her a lot.'

'So he told me. He also seemed a little bit disappointed to discover it wasn't you who would be treating him.'

Actually, more than a little disappointed, Ezra remembered, whereas his jaw had dropped when Greensay's reputedly wealthiest man had limped into his consulting room.

Brian Guthrie had to be fifty-five if he was a day, not to mention being red-cheeked, portly and balding. OK, so he knew that looks weren't everything, but if this was Mairi Morrison's idea of eligible manhood for Jess, he dreaded to think what Fraser Kennedy must look like.

Not that it was any of his business, of course, and neither did he care, but he'd have thought Jess deserved something better than a fifty-five-year-old with gout, or a wizened sailor.

'Jess—'

'The trouble is, people still tend to regard gout as a bit of a joke,' she observed, sipping her coffee pensively, 'and it's anything but for the poor sufferer. In fact, I believe it can lead to serious bone and kidney damage if it's not treated.'

'So the book you gave me said.' Ezra nodded. 'Thanks for the loan of it, by the way. Gout wasn't something I tended to come across when I—before I stopped practising medicine.'

Damn, but she wished he wouldn't do that, she thought with frustration. Almost reveal what branch of medicine he'd been in, then suddenly clam up. It was so *tantalising*. And there was no point in asking him. She'd already tried it and had got nowhere.

Anyway, he was a good doctor, and that was all she really needed to know, but she couldn't deny she was curious—OK, more than curious—about what he'd done before and why he didn't practise any more.

'I had another case of head lice in this morning,' she said, determinedly dragging her mind away from Ezra's past.

He smiled ruefully. 'Snap. Looks like it's going to go through the whole school. You'd better drop into the shop before you start on your home visits this afternoon and warn Nazir to stock up on antiseptic shampoo.'

She nodded and turned as Tracy popped her head round the staff room door.

'Morning mail's arrived, Doctors. Do you want it in here, or...?'

'In here's fine,' Jess answered, only to immediately regret her decision the minute when Tracy came in.

Heavens, but her skirt *was* short. Short and tight, revealing a pair of long, perfectly shaped slender thighs which tapered down into even more slender ankles. The kind of ankles any woman would have envied. The kind of legs to die for, Jess thought wistfully as the girl left the staffroom. Her legs had never been great even before she'd broken one. In fact, if she'd worn a skirt like that it wouldn't have been admiring glances she'd have drawn but laughter.

'Personally I prefer long skirts.'

Her head snapped round to Ezra in surprise. 'Do you?' she said before she could stop herself.

'Oh, yes. I'm a firm believer in the old adage that grown-up women shouldn't need to advertise their wares. Just as grown-up men prefer discovering them for themselves.'

He was smiling at her—a warm, understanding, half-quizzical smile—and to Jess's acute dismay she found herself blushing. Good grief, just because he'd paid her a compliment—at least, she thought he had—it was no reason for her to blush like a tomato.

It wasn't as though she was inexperienced. She'd had relationships with men in the past—well, all right, so she'd had precisely two boyfriends but surely that qualified her as being experienced? And other men had paid her compliments and never before had she blushed like a teenager. Or felt so unsettled, and edgy, and odd.

Ezra saw her confusion and cursed himself inwardly. What on earth had possessed him to say what he had? OK, so he'd meant it, but he'd already made up his mind to keep things on a strictly professional footing with Jess. And making personal comments about her appearance definitely wasn't keeping things on a professional level.

'Did I—?'

'Have you—?'

They'd spoken together, and to her chagrin Jess blushed even more. 'You first.'

'I was only going to say I've arranged for Colin McPhail to see the orthopaedic consultant on the mainland,' Ezra said quickly. 'He badly needs a hip replacement.'

That was more like it, she told herself, crushing down her quite irrational sense of disappointment at his abrupt change of conversation. Work. She should be concentrating on work, not on... Well, not on how somebody could look so completely different if they smiled in a particular way, or the strange and unsettling sensations that a simple smile could create.

'I agree with you,' she said quickly, 'but I'm afraid you've wasted your time, making an appointment for Colin. He won't have the operation.'

'Of course he will,' he protested.

'You mean, you've actually managed to convince him that his dogs will be OK?' she said, unable to conceal her amazement.

'His dogs?' he repeated in confusion, and she sighed.

'Ezra, Colin has three dogs and he's terrified they'll pine if he goes into hospital. And it's no good suggesting that a neighbour can look after them while he's away,' she added as he tried to interrupt. 'I've tried that, and it didn't work. He said he'd rather put up with the pain than abandon his friends.'

'Then why the hell didn't he tell me so when I suggested the operation to him?' he fumed. 'I've already rung the hospital, spoken to the consultant.'

She stared down at the dregs of her coffee, remembering Wattie's jibe and the comments of some of her other patients. 'Did you actually suggest it, Ezra, or did you simply tell him?'

'Of course I discussed it with him!' he exclaimed. 'I explained the operation in full, discussed all the pros and the cons, the success rate and the likely prognosis for long-term recovery, and he never once said anything about dogs.'

She doubted if she would have said very much when faced with Ezra in full professional mode. In fact, she doubted if she would have said anything at all.

'Ezra…' Oh, heavens, how to say this tactfully without offending him. 'Perhaps you didn't give him time to say anything. Perhaps you got a bit carried away with explaining the procedure…'

'Are you saying I bamboozled him with data?' he demanded, and she groaned inwardly.

Lord, this conversation was going from bad to worse, but she had to make him see, understand.

'Of course I'm not, but... Look, you were a hospital doctor before, weren't you?' she said, and saw his shoulders stiffen. Bingo! Well, that was one thing she now knew about him for sure. 'Sometimes—and I'm not saying you ever did this—but sometimes hospital doctors forget that people have minds of their own—agendas, wishes of their own—and aren't simply the sum total of their ailments or disease.'

He banged both their empty coffee-cups down onto the tray and angrily got to his feet. 'Now you're accusing me of not listening!'

'I'm not—truly, I'm not!' she replied. 'All I'm saying is it's very easy to get carried away with the technology of our profession, the wonderful things our skills can achieve, and if we're not careful we can start thinking we're gods, and—'

She didn't get the chance to finish. Ezra picked up the tray and began walking to the door when suddenly—and completely without warning—it slipped through his fingers, sending the cups crashing to the floor.

'Oh, hell, I'm sorry!' he gasped, staring down at the shattered remnants of their coffee-break. 'I'll pay for a new set...'

'Don't be silly. There's no need—'

'Of course there is!' he snapped, bending down and beginning to pick up the broken pieces of crockery. 'I broke them so I should replace them!'

'Ezra, it's two measly cups and saucers, not an entire set of Sèvres china!' she exclaimed, but he didn't reply, merely continued with his task, and he might well have collected every piece if she hadn't suddenly noticed with horror that drops of blood were staining the carpet. 'You've cut yourself!'

'It's nothing.'

'But you're bleeding!' she protested, getting awkwardly to her feet and hopping towards him. 'Let me see...'

'I told you, it's nothing,' he repeated, and when she tried to take his hand to see for herself, he swung round on her furiously. 'For God's sake, *leave me be*!'

Never had Jess heard him quite so angry, but what worried her more were the tiny beads of sweat on his forehead, the way his hands were shaking.

'Ezra... Ezra, are you OK?' she said with concern.

'Of course I'm OK!' he thundered, then bit his lip when she flinched. 'I'm fine...fine,' he repeated more calmly. 'Look, I'll just put a couple of Steri-Strips on this, and then we'd better make a start on your home visits or your patients will think we're lost.'

At the moment Jess didn't give a damn what her patients thought. 'Ezra—'

'Your phone's ringing,' he pointed out unnecessarily. 'I'll be waiting for you in the car when you're ready to go.'

And he was. A little edgy, a little uncomfortable, but he was there.

Leave it, Jess, she told herself as she got into his car. OK, so you're eaten up with curiosity, wondering why he reacted the way he did, but if you push too hard he might up and leave, and then how are you going to manage?

So she kept her tongue between her teeth and to her relief by the time they'd called in on Jeff Turner to change the dressing on his ulcerated leg, then checked on Tess MacPherson's new baby, some of Ezra's tension had eased. And when they stopped at the pharmacy to warn Nazir about stocking up on antiseptic shampoo, Ezra was actually able to laugh when Nazir dragged him across to admire his new internet equipment.

'He is a nice man, your Dr Dunbar,' Nazir's wife observed when Jess joined her at the counter, the joys of the internet holding no appeal for either woman. 'But not, I think, a very happy one.'

Jess stared at her, startled. 'What on earth makes you say that?'

Indira bent down to pick up her son Aziz who was holding up his chubby arms to her. 'When Nazir and I lived on the mainland I was not happy. Sometimes there was name-calling in the street—occasionally even stones thrown. Your Dr Dunbar—he has not the same reason to be unhappy, but he *is* unhappy. And I think, for him, no matter how far he runs, or how fast, the pain will remain.'

'Indira—'

'Jess, are you ready to go?' Ezra called from the shop door.

She wasn't—not by a long country mile. She wanted to ask Indira to explain, to tell her more, but Nazir's wife was already walking away, her colourful sari glinting in the winter sunshine.

Was Ezra unhappy? she wondered as he drove her out of Inverlairg. Sometimes she thought she saw shadows lurking in his deep grey eyes, as though he had memories which weren't very pleasant, but he didn't speak much about himself at all.

Taciturn, her father would have said. Brusque was how some of her patients described him, but she thought he was simply a man who kept his emotions on a tight rein. A man who couldn't open up to anyone, and yet who probably should.

And now she was psychoanalysing him, she realised with an inward groan, which was pretty rich considering she knew nothing about him.

But you'd like to know, wouldn't you? a little voice whispered at the back of her mind.

Well, of course she would, she retorted. Considering he was virtually her partner at the moment, it would have been more surprising if she *hadn't* been interested in his past.

And is it only his past you're interested in? the annoying

little voice asked with a chuckle, and she crushed it down with irritation.

She had more important things to think about anyway, she told herself firmly. Mairi Morrison, for one. Mairi, whose X-rays results had come back from the Sinclair Memorial three days ago and yet, despite Jess leaving repeated messages on her answering machine, still hadn't come down to the surgery to discuss them.

'I see you've brought the big guns with you this time,' Mairi said with resignation when she opened her front door and saw them standing there. 'Well, I suppose you'd better come in.'

'Mairi, if you'd rather Dr Dunbar waited in the car...'

'I don't much care one way or the other,' the woman sighed. 'Let's just get it over with.'

Ezra glanced across at Jess, his eyebrows raised, and she shook her head. Something told her this visit was going to be a difficult one, and she might need him.

She was right.

'It's cancer, isn't it?' Mairi said, after Jess had told her the X-rays had revealed a shadow on her lung. 'My father died of lung cancer when he was fifty-six. That's why I've never smoked—never even tried one.'

'Mairi, it could be anything,' Jess said gently. 'You could have a chest infection. You could simply have moved slightly when Bev took the X-ray. I'll ask her to take some more, and I'd like you to supply a sputum sample—'

'No.'

'But—'

'Jess, my father had exactly the same symptoms as I have—the bad cough, feeling tired all the time, being breathless, losing weight. Your father sent him for more X-rays, took samples, did tests. Then he went through months of agonising treatment, and it was all for nothing. He still died.'

'But you've got to at least let me find out if you *do* have lung cancer!' Jess protested. 'You can't simply refuse to have more X-rays or to give me a sputum sample. It's ridiculous—crazy—burying your head in the sand like this!'

'Jess.'

Ezra was shaking his head warningly at her, and she knew what he was thinking—that only a few hours earlier she'd taken him to task about patient rights—but this was Mairi, and she couldn't give in without a fight.

She had to. No matter what she or Ezra said, Mairi was adamant. There would be no more X-rays, and no sputum sample.

'How can she be so *stupid*?' Jess said vehemently when Ezra finally drove her away. 'OK, so there's a shadow on her lung, but even if it *is* cancer it may well be in the early stages when we can do something about it, and if it isn't cancer she's going to suffer years of uncertainty and fear for nothing!'

'Jess—'

'What am I going to do? She can be so stubborn at times, so pigheaded, and—'

'You're very fond of her,' he said softly, drawing his car to a halt and switching off the ignition.

She gazed out of the car at the dark fields beyond. 'Fond' didn't even come close to how she felt about Mairi.

'Mairi...She was my mother's best friend, and when my mother died shortly after my fifteenth birthday everybody on the island was wonderful, so sympathetic, but Mairi...' Jess swallowed the lump in her throat as she remembered. 'She was special. She took care of the day-to-day things that nobody else thought of. Made sense out of something that had no sense. Without her...'

He reached out and clasped her hand in his. His touch was warm, and solid, and infinitely comforting. 'I'm sure, when she's had time to think about it, she'll see sense.'

She wanted to believe him—she really wanted to—but she knew he didn't believe it any more than she did.

And her depression hadn't lifted even by the time they got back to her cottage.

Normally she looked forward to Thursdays. With no evening surgery it was her time to relax, but tonight she just couldn't settle. There was nothing she wanted to watch on television, her leg was aching quite badly and she felt edgy and sticky and uncomfortable.

'A long, hot bath might make you feel better,' Ezra observed, his eyes following her as she hobbled awkwardly back from the bookcase, empty-handed. 'I could wrap a plastic bag round your cast and if you stuck your leg out over the side of the bath, it shouldn't get wet.'

A bath sounded wonderful. A real, proper bath instead of the cursory sponge job she'd been making do with, but... 'I'm afraid I don't think I could even get *in* the bath, Ezra, far less out again.'

'You could if I helped you.'

Was he serious? Good grief, he appeared to be, and Jess shook her head quickly. 'Thanks for the offer, but I don't think so.'

'Why ever not?' he protested. 'What's the problem?'

Apart from the fact that he was a man, she was a woman and the thought of him seeing her in all her too imperfect glory was making her toes curl with embarrassment?

'I'm not that bothered about a bath anyway,' she lied, fighting desperately with her mounting colour. 'I've masses of paperwork I need to catch up on and—'

'It's because I'm a man, isn't it?' he interrupted impatiently. 'If I were a woman, you'd have accepted like a shot.'

'OK. All right—I would,' she retorted before she could stop herself. 'Call me old-fashioned and prudish if you like, but I don't normally allow men I scarcely know to see me with nothing on!'

He drummed his fingers on the coffee-table, a deep frown creasing his forehead. 'Right, we have a problem here, but we're both mature, intelligent people and there has to be a way round it.'

'Ezra, it doesn't matter—'

'If you had a shower instead of a bath we wouldn't have this problem,' he continued as though she hadn't spoken. 'Mind you, the plastic bag on your leg would get soaked, and...' He came to a sudden halt, his eyes lighting up. 'Of course. A shower—it's obvious!'

'But I haven't got one,' she said in confusion.

'No, but you've got a shower cap.'

'A shower cap?' she echoed, as he put his hand firmly under her arm and helped her out of the sitting room and into the bathroom. 'Ezra, how in the world will a shower cap help?'

'Like this,' he announced triumphantly, whipping her plastic shower cap off the back of the bathroom door, putting it on his head and pulling it down over his eyes. 'Wearing this I can help you in and out of the bath, and your modesty is preserved.'

She stared at him, bemused. 'Ezra, that's a ridiculous idea!'

He pushed the bath cap up so it sat at a rakish angle on his head. 'Perhaps, but it will work.'

'But...' She could feel her cheeks heating up all over again. 'I'm sure you mean well—in fact, I know you do—but...'

'Look, would an oath satisfy you?' he said in exasperation, and before she could answer he'd drawn himself up to his full six feet two, raised his hand high in the air and begun intoning gravely, 'I, Ezra Dunbar, do solemnly swear that this shower cap will remain over my eyes when I help Jess Arden in and out of her bath. There will be no peeking, peeping or any other underhanded attempt to look at her body.' He lowered his hand and frowned. 'Satisfied?'

She giggled—she couldn't help it. He looked so silly wearing her shower cap. Silly, and kind, and eager to help. Before she'd even had time to think about it she heard herself say, 'OK.'

It was better than OK. It was bliss. Bliss to feel the warm water enclosing her, even if it was awkward sitting with her right leg propped out over the side. Bliss to feel really clean at last instead of merely half-washed.

And Ezra...

He sat perched on the toilet seat in case she slipped, and decided he must have been out of his mind.

What on earth had ever made him suggest this?

OK, so she'd looked unhappy and he'd wanted to help, but in the cold light of day he knew he would never have suggested it. In the cold light of day he would have thought it through and realised he couldn't possibly lift her into the bath without touching her naked body.

He knew it now. Knew how soft and warm her skin was. Knew the way her waist curved gently inwards, the fullness of her bottom and how ripe her breasts were because his fingers had accidentally brushed against one as he'd lowered her into the bath.

It didn't matter that he couldn't see anything. Having felt all her warm softness, he could imagine. Hell, but he'd never realised he possessed such a vivid imagination, and it was working overtime.

'Are you OK?' she asked as he shifted uncomfortably on the toilet.

'I'm...um...fine,' he managed to reply, tugging slightly at his shirt collar, only to hear the sound of water splashing as though she'd levered herself upright. Had levered that luscious, soft, warm body upright. 'Are *you* OK?' he asked quickly.

'Wonderful,' she murmured with a contented sigh, which did nothing for his equilibrium.

It was crazy. Just one short week ago he'd decided Jess Arden was the most irritatingly stubborn woman he'd ever met, so why on earth was he finding himself wanting her now?

Lust, of course. The fact that, though his brain had sense, his body had none, and it was simply rampantly reminding him that he hadn't made love to a woman for more than a year.

Which didn't mean he had to give into his body's demands, and he wouldn't. Right now Jess needed him to keep her practice running, and to abuse that need would be unforgivable.

So, like a perfect gentleman, he would control his libido until the locum arrived, and then he'd leave. Leave the practice, leave the island, and never once remember a girl with stunning red hair and skin which was as soft and smooth as velvet.

'I'm ready to get out now, Ezra.'

So was he, but he still had four weeks to go. Four long, interminable weeks. As he gritted his teeth and prepared to lift Jess out of the bath, he could only hope his blood pressure would stand it.

CHAPTER FOUR

CATH STEWART smiled as she stood beside Jess in the car park and watched Ezra help old Mr Dean into the health centre. 'Tracy's right, you know. Ezra *is* nice.'

He was.

Nice and kind and even after two weeks of living and working with him, still a completely unknown quantity to her, Jess thought with a slight sigh.

'I wonder why he came to Greensay?' Cath continued, unconsciously echoing her thoughts. 'I mean, apart from the fact that nobody in their right mind would choose to come here in the middle of winter, what kind of job would give him three months' holiday?'

Jess had wondered about that, too. Wondered increasingly since Indira's comment last week.

'Perhaps he writes books for a living,' she murmured, as much to herself as to her receptionist. 'And he came to Greensay looking for peace and quiet to finish a book.'

Cath frowned as she chained her bicycle to the railing. 'Wattie said he didn't notice him unloading anything even faintly resembling a laptop from his car when he moved into Selkie Cottage.'

'I'm surprised he didn't go through Ezra's suitcases just to make sure,' Jess said tightly, hitching her crutches up under her arms and beginning to hop across the car park to the Inverlairg Health Centre. 'Honestly, that man—doesn't he ever give up?'

'Doesn't look like it,' Cath replied. 'Mind you, if you want real, dogged determination you don't have to look much further than my daughter.'

'Rebecca still being difficult?' Jess asked sympathetically, and Cath rolled her eyes heavenwards.

'*Difficult?* Ever since she hit fourteen, I've become an
idiot and she knows everything.'

'I seem to remember being much the same at that age,'
Jess laughed, but Cath didn't.

'It's so damn wearing, Jess. Perhaps if I spent more time
with her, perhaps if Peter was home, but...' She shook her
head. 'He phoned me last night—said he was doing fine,
but longing for March, like me.'

Jess nodded. Cath's husband worked in the oil industry
and could only come home twice a year to see his wife and
daughter. It was a lonely life for Cath but, as Peter had
said, he had to go where the work was.

'How are you getting on, having Ezra as a lodger?' Cath
continued, holding open the surgery door to let Jess hop in
ahead of her. 'It must feel really odd after being on your
own for the last three years.'

Actually it didn't, Jess realised with a sudden shock. It
was nice. Nice to buy for two instead of one. Nice to have
someone to talk to at the end of the day. Nice to look up
in the middle of a meal and see someone there.

'It would be wonderful, wouldn't it, if Ezra decided to
stay on here permanently?' Cath commented, watching her,
and Jess shook her head.

'Cath, there's scarcely enough people on Greensay to
warrant my salary, far less another doctor's.'

'I wasn't actually thinking of him staying on as a doctor,'
the receptionist murmured. 'I was thinking more...well,
more on the lines of maybe you and Ezra getting together.'

'Now, hold on there a moment—'

'Jess, he's perfect for you,' Cath exclaimed in a rush.
'Good-looking—'

'How can you tell with that beard?'

'Intelligent, kind—'

'And here on holiday,' Jess interrupted firmly. 'The min-

ute my locum arrives he'll disappear back to Selkie Cottage
and I guarantee we'll never see him again.'

For a second Cath looked disconcerted, then rallied. 'But
he likes you,' she protested, lowering her voice quickly
when the clatter of high heels on the tarmac outside the
surgery announced Tracy's imminent arrival. 'I know he
does. And you like him—'

'And as I recall, this is your mums and toddlers morning,' Jess declared, 'so you'd better don your practice
nurse's hat pronto before they start arriving.'

That Cath would dearly like to continue the conversation
was obvious, but what could Jess say? Yes, she liked him.
More than she would have thought possible two weeks ago,
but as for him liking her...

Not by a word or a look had he ever suggested he regarded her as anything but a colleague. Good grief, he'd
even helped her in and out of the bath last week and still
behaved like a perfect gentleman.

Actually, he'd been so much of a perfect gentleman it
was a bit depressing. OK, so maybe she wasn't ever going
to win any beauty contests, and maybe she was rather more
rounded—well, all right, then, plump—than was currently
fashionable, but...

But nothing, she told herself. Good grief, it wasn't as
though she was interested in the man in the sense of being
interested. She'd never liked beards, had always thought
they made men look scruffy no matter how well trimmed
they were. And just because she'd recently found herself
wondering what it would feel like to be kissed by a man
with a beard, that meant nothing. It *didn't*.

'Doctor, help—I need some help here!' Danny Hislop
cried, shattering her thoughts in an instant when he shouldered open the surgery door. She saw Simon Ralston beside
him, his hand swathed in a bloodstained towel.

'Tracy, you take over the desk and warn everyone who
arrives we're going to be running late,' Jess ordered as the
girl stared at Simon in stunned horror. 'Danny, keep

Simon's hand up as high as you can. Cath, treatment room—now!'

'I don't know how it happened, Doc,' Danny declared, his face almost as white as his friend's as he and Cath helped Simon along to the treatment room while Jess followed more slowly, inwardly cursing her crutches. 'We were coming back to harbour in *The Aurora*, and the captain says let's give it one last try for a decent catch, and somehow…somehow Simon's hand got caught in the hawser.'

Jess winced. The hawser was the cable used to pull the fishing net to the side of the ship. It was made of metal, and moved at a terrifying speed, and if Simon's hand had been caught in that…

'How long ago did this happen?' she asked, propping her crutches against the wall while Cath began taking Simon's blood pressure and pulse.

'Thirty—forty minutes ago,' Danny replied. 'We got him back to shore as quickly as we could.'

'BP 130 over 90,' Cath announced. 'Pulse 135.'

Both surprisingly good, considering the injury Simon had sustained, and thankfully somebody on *The Aurora* had possessed the presence of mind to tie a towel tightly round his hand to minimise the blood loss. But the more Jess swabbed his hand, the more her heart sank.

Lord, but it was a mess. The wound was deep. Deep and ragged and extensive.

Cath was watching her, and Jess knew what she was thinking. He needed a specialist. She could stitch quite large wounds—had happily done so in the past—but if she got this one wrong Simon could lose all mobility in his hand.

'Simon…' He was looking distinctly green, and she reached for a bowl just in case. 'Simon, I'm sorry, but I think we should call out the lifeboat—have you transferred to the mainland. That hand—it should be seen by an expert.'

He shook his head vehemently. 'Doctor, you know what my wife's like. She's already worried to death about Toby—him having this juvenile arthritis thing—and if I go off and leave her...'

Elspeth would fall apart. The unspoken words hung between them, but though Jess felt sorry for Simon's wife she knew she couldn't take the risk.

'Simon, I'm really sorry, but—'

'Is there a problem?'

Ezra was standing in the doorway of the treatment room and she nodded grimly. 'Simon got his hand caught in the hawser, and I'm just telling him he needs someone with far greater skills than I possess to stitch it.'

Quickly he walked across the room and lifted Simon's hand in his. 'Nasty. Very nasty,' he murmured, 'but I could stitch it for you.'

'Then do it,' Simon exclaimed eagerly, but Ezra was no longer looking at him. His eyes were resting on Jess.

'It's your call,' he said softly. 'I *can* do it, but if you'd feel happier—safer—sending him to the mainland...'

Two weeks ago all she'd known about this man was that he'd once been a doctor, and yet she'd allowed him to become a member of her practice. Good grief, she even allowed him to do half of her home visits now—liberally armed with the necessary patient files, of course—but to let him tackle this...

She'd have to be crazy. Crazy to allow a man she knew so little about perform such a difficult procedure. If he got it wrong...

But he wouldn't get it wrong. As his eyes held hers she knew that he wouldn't, and she turned to Simon with a smile. 'It looks like you're staying put after all.'

The fisherman let out a huge sigh of relief, but Ezra wasn't listening. He was already snapping on a pair of surgical gloves.

'OK, Cath. I'll need lignocaine to numb the hand, a pair

of toothed dissecting forceps, your finest needles and a wire brush.'

'A wire brush?' she repeated in confusion, and he nodded.

'If you don't get all the dirt out from a wound like this, not only will it become infected, the dirt will become permanently tattooed into the skin. That's why I need a wire brush—to scour out all the dirt. If you haven't got a brush I can use a teaspoon to dig out any residual dirt. A well-sterilised teaspoon, of course,' he added.

Cath glanced across at Jess, her eyebrows raised queryingly but Jess merely nodded.

Ezra was a pro. She'd suspected it even before he began wielding the teaspoon as though it were the finest surgical instrument in the world. And she knew it for certain once he began suturing with a speed which was breathtaking.

This man had been a surgeon for sure, but in what speciality, and why he would turn his back on such a talent was beyond her.

'I think I can finish off here now if the two of you want to get back to your patients,' Cath declared when Ezra had finally tied the last suture in place.

'Are you sure?' Ezra said uncertainly, and the receptionist laughed.

'Look, if you can perform miracles with a teaspoon, I sure as heck can put on a surgical pad and bandage!'

He laughed, too, but as he made for the door Jess put out her hand to stop him.

'I just...' She came to a halt. There was so much she wanted to say. That his skill was amazing. That he'd saved both Simon and Elspeth a lot of grief and heartbreak. But as he stared down at her, his grey eyes suddenly wary, the only words which came out were, 'Thank you.'

Which was really dumb, of course, and totally inadequate, but Ezra didn't seem to think so.

The wariness in his eyes disappeared, and his lips curved into a smile. 'Any time, Jess.'

Which was the sort of casual, offhand thing people often said at a time like this, so why, as he continued to gaze down at her, should her heart begin to perform the most peculiar back flips in her chest?

Men with beards were chinless wonders. Men with beards had never been—could never be—her type. And yet as his eyes held hers all she was aware of was how breathless she felt, and bewildered, and strangely expectant. Like her life had somehow started to begin. Which was *crazy*.

'Dr Arden—Dr Dunbar?'

The voice was impatient, a little querulous, suggesting that Simon had been attempting to attract their attention for quite some time, and Jess turned to him quickly, all too conscious her cheeks must be flushed.

'Simon wants to know when his sutures can come out,' Cath said, her eyes darting from Jess to Ezra and back again with keen interest.

'In about ten days,' Ezra said abruptly. 'But I'm afraid you're not going to be fit for work for at least six weeks.'

Simon's jaw dropped. 'But I can't take six weeks off work! The boss will need to hire someone to replace me on the boat, and what if he decides to keep him on?'

'Your boss can't sack you when you've suffered an industrial injury,' Ezra pointed out. 'You could take him to an industrial tribunal if he did.'

'Yes, but he could relegate me to shore duties, which means I'd lose my bonuses. And he'd do it, too,' Simon continued when Ezra tried to interrupt. 'My work's not been up to scratch lately, you see, what with all this worry about Toby.'

'I'm sorry, but there's no way you're going to be fit for work in less than six weeks,' Ezra declared. 'And now, if you'll excuse me…'

He was already leaving the treatment room and Simon turned to Jess desperately. 'Couldn't I wear some sort of protective glove? I'm sure if I wore something like that I could keep on fishing.'

For a second Jess's eyes followed Ezra, then she willed herself to concentrate on the fisherman's problems. 'Have you told your boss about your family difficulties?'

'Fraser doesn't listen much to anyone these days,' Danny replied before Simon could say anything. 'In fact, he's a real pain in the ar—the butt.'

'Fraser?' Jess repeated, her brain suddenly acute and alert. '*The Aurora*'s one of Fraser Kennedy's boats?'

Danny nodded, and a frown creased Jess's forehead.

It didn't sound at all like the Fraser she knew. In fact, if anyone had asked her opinion she'd have said he was one of the most laid-back men on the island.

'Cath, doesn't Fraser have an appointment with Dr Dunbar this morning?'

'Nine-thirty, as I recall.'

'Right. I'll have a word with him,' Jess declared determinedly, and saw blind panic appear in Simon's eyes.

'Doc, please, don't make waves. I don't want to lose my job completely.'

'You won't,' she replied.

And he wouldn't. OK, so her conversations with Fraser had been limited to a passing greeting recently, but he couldn't have changed all that much since they'd last had a proper talk. She would simply explain the situation, he'd understand and that would be an end to the matter.

In fact, probably the hardest thing would be getting a chance to speak to him. Simon's accident must have shot their appointment system to bits, and there was every likelihood that Fraser had got tired of waiting and left.

He hadn't. In fact, he was the first person she saw when she returned to the waiting room, but if she was delighted to see him, Fraser looked anything but pleased to see her.

'My appointment's with Dr Dunbar, Jess,' he declared firmly when she hopped towards him. 'I specifically asked to see Dr Dunbar.'

'*Ooh*, but he's going all red,' said one of the young mums waiting for Cath's Monday babies and toddlers clinic. 'What's wrong with you, then, Fraser, that you're no' wanting a woman to examine you?'

'Button your lip, Effie Hamilton!' he snapped back. 'Unless you're wanting everyone to know what you got up to at summer camp when you were fifteen!'

The other mums in the waiting room most certainly wanted to know and as the unfortunate Effie subsided in her seat under a barrage of eager questions, Jess quickly urged Fraser out into the corridor.

'I only want to *talk* to you,' she said when he began protesting again. 'It's about one of your men—Simon Ralston. He got his hand caught in the hawser of *The Aurora* this morning, and Dr Dunbar's told him he can't return to work for at least six weeks.'

Fraser swore under his breath. 'The idiot! The man's a complete waste of space. His mind's never on his job—'

'Fraser, his son has juvenile arthritis.'

'And we've all got problems, but the rest of us don't let them interfere with our work,' he retorted. 'Because he's injured I'm going to have to put him on shore duties and hire someone else for *The Aurora*, which will mean more expense!'

'Fraser—'

'Actually, it might not be such a disaster after all,' he continued thoughtfully. 'I've been wanting to get rid of him for ages, and if I keep him on shore duties long enough, maybe he'll get so bored he'll simply resign.'

'But that would be a wicked thing to do!' she exclaimed.

'Jess, fishing's a tough business. I can't carry passengers.'

Her green eyes flashed fire. 'Oh, really? Well, in that case you won't mind if I tell PC Inglis about the special passengers you were carrying in the back of your Range Rover last Thursday night. The duty-free wine and cigarettes?'

'How the hell did you find—?'

'I've got my sources, Fraser,' she interrupted, only to

redden when she suddenly realised that Ezra was helping old Mrs Mackay out of his consulting room. Mrs Mackay was, thankfully, very deaf. Ezra unfortunately wasn't. Not from the way his eyebrows shot up. 'Look,' she continued in an acid undertone as Ezra escorted Mrs Mackay back to the waiting room, 'Simon's got family trouble right now, and all I'm saying is if you give him a little leeway, my lips will remain sealed about your contraband.'

For a moment Fraser said nothing, then he smiled grimly. 'You drive a hard bargain, Jess.'

'I want to know why I've got to make one at all,' she protested. 'You're not normally so unsympathetic, so grouchy. Are you in pain—is that why you want to see Dr Dunbar?'

The colour on his cheeks returned. 'Yes, I'm in pain, but it's...well, the pain's in a very personal place.'

'Fraser, I'm a doctor. There's nothing I haven't seen—'

'Look, I've got piles, OK?' he interrupted, scarlet-cheeked. 'Which is why I'm damned if I'll let you examine me. Hell, Jess, we've dated, kissed—'

'I'm ready for you now, Mr Kennedy,' Ezra declared, his voice clipped, and to Jess's annoyance the two men disappeared into Ezra's consulting room before she'd had the chance to point out that it must be two years at least since she'd been out on a date with Fraser.

Not that it mattered, of course. She could date whoever she liked—kiss whoever she liked—and yet...

She still wished Fraser hadn't said it, and then was angry with herself for the wish. What difference did it make, anyway? She very much doubted if Ezra was even remotely interested.

Ezra was actually very interested. In fact, as he sat down behind his desk and stared at the man sitting opposite him, he experienced something he had never felt before. A stab of quite unreasonable, irrational jealousy.

Brian Guthrie had been one thing. The portly, balding farmer was obviously a complete non-starter, but Fraser

Kennedy... He was thirty-three, according to his patient file, tall, muscular and good-looking if your taste ran to blue-eyed blonds, which he understood quite a lot of women's did.

Jess's taste clearly did if she'd been dating him. And much as he longed to accuse her of having rotten taste, he couldn't. OK, so the bloke apparently dealt in contraband, but he suspected there were precious few fishermen on the island who didn't bring back the odd bottle from their trips abroad. If Fraser Kennedy *did* have haemorrhoids he obviously didn't take enough roughage in his diet, but neither of these things disqualified him from being a suitable husband for Jess. And to Ezra's annoyance he discovered he desperately wanted something to disqualify him.

'I've always had a bit of bother in that region, Doc—having to strain when I go,' Fraser was saying with embarrassment. 'But this last six months...I'm in agony all the time.'

'Is the bleeding profuse when you pass a stool, or very dark in colour?' Ezra asked, forcing himself to concentrate.

Fraser shook his head. 'It's just a little bit of blood, and it isn't dark. More bright red, in fact.'

'Any pain in your abdomen, or persistent pain in the anal area?' Ezra persisted. Another shake of the head. As Fraser wasn't over fifty and there didn't appear to have been any marked change in his bowel habit, it didn't look as though he was suffering from anything sinister. 'OK, could you slip down your trousers for me?'

And while I examine you I can wonder what the hell I'm doing, vetting Jess Arden's potential husbands, Ezra thought, angrily snapping on a pair of surgical gloves. Her love life was nothing to do with him. If she wanted to marry Wattie Hope, it would still have nothing to do with him.

He was getting too involved, that was the trouble. He should have ignored her wan face and large green eyes, and taken his chances with the police. If he'd done that he wouldn't now be treating the kind of cases he hadn't seen since his pre-registration days, and he wouldn't have found himself getting increasingly sucked into Jess's life.

And he didn't want to become involved in her life. Lusting after her warm, luscious body was one thing—he would simply have to control his libido for another three weeks—but starting to care about what happened to her... That was far too dangerous for both of them.

'Can you do something about them, Doc?' Fraser asked once Ezra had confirmed that the fisherman did indeed have haemorrhoids. 'I've tried sitting in warm baths to ease the pain—'

'Which was actually the worst thing you could have done,' Ezra interrupted. 'Taking a warm bath softens the skin, you see, allowing the water to pass through the haemorrhoid so the swelling actually gets bigger. Warm baths only help if you add a handful of salt to them. That soothes the area and reduces the swelling.'

'And is that all the help you can offer—chuck some salt into a bath?' Fraser protested. 'Doc, I can't sit—can hardly walk—and as for going to the loo...!'

'I'll give you a tube of antiseptic cream, which should ease the pain,' Ezra said calmly, 'but what you really need is a small operation.'

'An operation?' Fraser echoed, paling visibly.

'It's not a complicated procedure. We'd use an instrument called a proctoscope, which places tight bands round each individual haemorrhoid so that they wither and drop off after a few days. It doesn't hurt,' he added, seeing Fraser gulp. 'In fact, you can have it done as an outpatient without the need for anaesthetic. I'll make an appointment for you at the Sinclair Memorial, and Dr Arden—'

'Couldn't you do it for me, Doc?' Fraser interrupted, and Ezra's heart sank.

A year ago he would have laughed if anyone had said he might have to think twice about removing someone's haemorrhoids, but now...

And yet how could he refuse? If he did, Jess would want

to know why. Hell, he could tell she was already eaten up with curiosity, and her brain must be working overtime now she'd seen him suture Simon Ralston's hand.

'I'll make you an appointment for the operation at the hospital,' he replied evenly, 'but I can't guarantee it will be quick.' In fact, he was going to make damn sure it wasn't so that either Jess or the locum would eventually have to do the procedure. 'In the meantime, keep using the antiseptic cream.'

'Thanks, Doc,' Fraser said fervently. 'I guess it's stupid, not wanting Jess to do it, but we—well, we're friends, if you know what I mean.'

Unfortunately Ezra rather thought he did when he escorted Fraser back to the waiting room and saw the smile the big fisherman flashed at Jess.

Three more weeks he told himself grimly. He only had three more weeks of this to endure, and then he could leave Greensay, forget about Jess Arden and get on with his life. The fact that he felt an overwhelming desire to punch Fraser on the nose meant nothing. All it meant was that living with a very attractive woman on a strictly platonic basis was an incredibly bad idea for any normal, healthy male.

'Ezra doesn't look too happy,' Tracy said curiously, as he disappeared back into his consulting room. 'I'd have thought he'd be doing high fives after stitching Simon Ralston's hand.'

Jess thought he would have too. In fact, she wanted some answers, and fully intended getting them, but not right now. Not with Robb MacGregor walking towards her, looking white, drawn and downright miserable.

'I've got diarrhoea now, Doctor,' he said as soon as they were alone. 'And my stomach's hurting like hell no matter what I eat.'

'Have you noticed whether your stools are much blacker than usual when you go to the bathroom?'

He nodded, and Jess reached for her stethoscope. Diarrhoea, stomach pain and dark stools. With symptoms like these it seemed they were finally getting somewhere. Robb clearly thought they were, too, but not in a way Jess would have wished.

'I…I was reading an article in one of my wife's magazines last night,' he began uncertainly. 'It said if you were tired all the time, and had weight loss, sickness and diarrhoea, you could have bowel cancer.'

Jess bit back the oath which sprang to her lips and angrily stabbed the ends of her stethoscope into her ears. Magazine articles were the bane of her life—as were medical series on the television. OK, so they were occasionally very useful—alerting people to conditions they might otherwise have ignored—but they could also cause quite unnecessary fear and panic.

Which she was sure they had done by the time she'd finished examining Robb.

'I think you've got a peptic ulcer,' she observed. 'I'll make you an appointment at the infirmary to confirm it, but I'm pretty sure that's what you've got.'

She expected him to argue, to say he couldn't possibly leave his business for a whole day to go to the mainland, but he merely accepted the antacid she gave him and left without a word.

'Honestly, Cath, I'm all for educating the public,' she complained when the receptionist brought in her coffee after morning surgery, 'but why does everybody always automatically think they have cancer? First it's Mairi, and now it's Robb.'

'I suppose it's what everybody's most afraid of,' her receptionist murmured. 'The C word.'

'Yes, but do you remember the talk I gave on breast cancer at the Women's Institute—when I said nine out of the ten lumps which women find in their breasts generally turn out to be non-malignant? Well, it's the same with most cancer scares. Quite often they turn out to be false alarms.'

Cath picked up the patient files on Jess's desk, put them

down again and cleared her throat. 'Jess, about that talk you gave…'

She came to a halt as the phone on Jess's desk rang, and with an apologetic smile Jess stretched out to answer it, only to immediately wish she hadn't.

'I'm sorry, Bev, but I'm afraid I've got nowhere with Mairi,' she was forced to tell the radiographer. 'Yes, I do appreciate how tight your schedule is nowadays, but…'

'I don't see how you're going to persuade Mairi to have more X-rays if she's really dug in her heels,' Cath said when Jess finally replaced the receiver.

'Neither do I,' Jess murmured, then straightened up in her seat with an effort. 'I'm sorry, Cath. What were you saying to me before?'

Her receptionist opened her mouth, then closed it again as Ezra strode into the consulting room and made a beeline for the coffee.

'You've no idea how much I've been looking forward to this,' he exclaimed, lifting one of the coffee-cups, only to glance from Cath to Jess, then back again. 'Sorry. Am I interrupting something?'

Cath shook her head and smiled. 'It's nothing—nothing important anyway.'

Ezra frowned as the receptionist hurried away. 'Why do I get the feeling she's lying?'

'I'm just hoping she wasn't trying to pluck up the courage to tell me she wants to resign. She's got family problems at the moment, you see,' Jess explained, seeing Ezra's eyebrows shoot up, 'and being both my receptionist and the practice nurse… It's too much. That's why I hired Tracy— to spread the load—but until she learns the ropes, all I've done is add another burden.'

'And I'm afraid I've got another one to add,' he said, sitting down. 'Ruth Bain has measles.'

Jess dragged her fingers through her red curls and groaned. 'Oh, terrific! Half the school's already down with head lice, and now I bet you anything we've got an out-break of measles to look forward to.'

'I was surprised to learn she hadn't been immunised against it,' Ezra said, and Jess sighed.

'We had a much better take-up rate when it was a sep-arate vaccination, but ever since it was suggested that the MMR vaccine might cause or contribute to autism, I've had the devil's own job to get mums to agree to their children having it.'

Ezra nodded. 'I guess parents have to weigh up the pos-sible *known* consequences of contracting measles—enceph-alitis, ear and lung infections and bacterial infection of the larynx—with the remote possibility their child might de-velop autism.'

'Yes, and because I don't have children it makes it dou-bly difficult for me to be convincing,' she declared. 'I get the ''Oh, it's all very well for you, Doctor, but you haven't got kids'' argument.'

She should have children, he thought. Two girls and a boy. Two girls who would look exactly like her, while the boy… His fingers tightened round his cup as the little boy he'd been imagining suddenly developed an uncanny re-semblance to Fraser Kennedy.

'Have you ever thought of having children?' he asked before he could stop himself, and saw her smile.

'Perhaps some time in the future, when I'm more estab-lished, but at the moment I'm happy as I am. I'm so lucky, you see, to be living here, doing a job that I love, and I keep thinking what more could I want?'

For a second he was tempted to tell her to stick to that view, to forget all about children—especially children who looked like Fraser Kennedy—but he couldn't. Not when he knew what could happen to a doctor who lived solely for work.

'How about getting yourself a life, for a start?' he said, and she laughed.

'But I've got one. I just told you—'

'I mean a *proper* life,' he interrupted. 'A life that doesn't consist solely of trying to fill your father's shoes.'

The laughter on her face died. 'I can't think of anyone's shoes I'd rather fill. My father was the most talented GP I've ever known. He was a legend on this island. He—'

'Was a saint.' Ezra nodded, trying—and failing—to keep the edge out of his voice. 'I'm sure he was, but saints generally get martyred, and I think you deserve something better than spending the rest of your life attempting to become a carbon copy of a man who—let's face it—probably wouldn't be able to cope with the pressures a GP faces nowadays.'

'You don't know anything about me, or my father!' she flared. 'Two weeks—that's all you've known me—and yet you presume to judge—'

'Jess, I'm not judging you, I'm trying to *help* you,' he interrupted impatiently. 'You're a good doctor. Be happy with that. Start living for yourself instead of grinding yourself into the ground, trying to become something you can never be.'

'And I think that's pretty rich, coming from someone who obviously used to be a surgeon but presumably couldn't hack it!' she threw back at him. 'At least I've got a goal, a purpose in life, and unlike you I've no intention of throwing in the towel just because things might be a little tough!'

The second the words were out of her mouth she wished them back. He couldn't have whitened more if she'd actually hit him, but it was the look in his eyes which had her struggling to her feet, full of remorse.

'Ezra, I'm sorry. What I said was unforgivable. I had no right—'

'Actually, you did.' He put down his coffee-cup, and his mouth twisted into a sad travesty of a smile. 'Because you're right. I couldn't hack it as a surgeon. I did throw in the towel.'

'Ezra—'

'I'm late for my home visits.' He walked slowly towards the door, and she saw with dismay that his shoulders were hunched, just as they'd been the first time she'd seen him walking along the beach. 'My list seems pretty straightforward, but if I meet any problems I'll let you know.'

'Ezra, don't go—wait!'

But he didn't wait, and when she heard his footsteps fading down the corridor she slumped back in her seat and put her head in her hands. Why had she said what she had? He'd looked so broken, as though she'd rubbed salt into an open wound. OK, so she didn't agree with what he'd said about her father, or his criticisms about how she lived her life, but he'd probably spoken with the best of intentions, and how had she repaid him?

By being cruel. By being cruel, and *wrong*. A man like Ezra Dunbar would never simply have thrown in the towel. He was a focused, dedicated, gifted doctor. Something catastrophic must have happened to make him give up medicine, but *what*?

CHAPTER FIVE

'JESS, tell me to mind my own business if you want,' Cath said as she put a pile of patient files down on Jess's desk, 'but have you and Ezra had a row?'

Jess clicked the save icon on her computer and sat back in her chair uncomfortably. 'Not a row as such. I—well, I sort of lost my temper a bit.' Which had to be the biggest understatement of the year. 'Said something I shouldn't.'

'Then can't you simply apologise?' her receptionist asked, her forehead creasing into an unhappy frown. 'There's been such an odd atmosphere in the surgery this week. I don't mean it's frosty or unpleasant, it's just...' She shook her head impotently. 'I'm sorry, but I can't explain it.'

Jess could, and if walking over broken glass would have turned the clock back she'd willingly have done it, but nothing would help.

She'd repeated her apology to Ezra the minute he'd come back from his home visits, but he'd dismissed her words as completely unnecessary. He'd even apologised to her—saying he shouldn't have tried to interfere in her life—but nothing had helped. The words she'd hurled at him were still there. Too cruel and hurtful to be erased.

'Make your peace with him, Jess,' Cath continued, her brown eyes worried, earnest. 'Don't go losing him because of a stupid argument.'

Losing him? Jess gazed at her receptionist in disbelief. Was she serious? She obviously was.

'Cath, read my lips. Ezra and I are colleagues. Nothing more, nothing less.'

'But I've seen the way you look at him—'

'And I think it's high time you got back to work if all you can do is stand there and talk utter nonsense!'

The receptionist blinked, crimsoned, looked as though she was about to burst into tears and then dashed out of the consulting room, leaving Jess gazing heavenwards with a mixture of anger and regret.

She hadn't meant to be quite so sharp, but did her receptionist really think she wanted to know that her growing interest in Ezra was obvious? It was bad enough that it was *there*, without someone commenting on something which was as inexplicable as it was ridiculous.

And it *was* ridiculous. What did she know about him? Nothing. What had he told her about himself? Next to nothing. He could have a wife and three kids in London, for all she knew. Dammit, he could be a serial bigamist, a five-times-married divorcé.

Quickly she pulled her keyboard towards her, only to push it away again with vexation. What in the world was wrong with her?

Just three short weeks ago she'd had her future all mapped out. And yet now, just because a mysterious, attractive stranger—OK, she admitted it, he *was* attractive—had come into her life, all her old certainty had gone. And for what?

A man who treated her with punctilious correctness. A man who could happily help her in and out of baths without batting an eye. Well, all right, so he'd only done it once and had never offered again, but that was beside the point. No, actually, it wasn't. It was *exactly* the point. It proved he wasn't interested in her. It proved he was merely counting the days until he could leave.

But what about that moment after he'd stitched Simon Ralston's hand? her mind whispered. That moment when he gazed at you and...

'Yeah, right,' she muttered. 'What about it?'

He hadn't been the one who'd got all flustered and confused. *His* cheeks hadn't glowed like twin beetroots. It had been *she* who'd behaved like a prize booby. And then—just to make absolutely sure he'd never be interested in her in a million years—what had she done? Gone and told him he couldn't hack it as a surgeon.

'Brilliant, Jess,' she sighed. 'Really brilliant. When you set out to capture a man's interest, you sure pick a terrific way of doing it.'

And sitting here, feeling stupid, when you've got a waiting room full of patients is pointless, she told herself as her consulting-room door opened and Tracy appeared.

'Jess, you're *never* going to believe who's just walked into the waiting room!'

'George Clooney?' she suggested hopefully, and Tracy laughed.

'Don't I just wish! But it's almost as good. Mairi Morrison.'

'You're kidding,' Jess gasped.

Tracy shook her head, all too aware of the number of phone calls Jess had made in an attempt to achieve just this moment. 'She's here, and she wants to know if you can possibly see her this morning.'

Jess couldn't—not really—but there was no way she was going to let Mairi leave without talking to her.

'Who's next on my list?'

'Mrs Wells, but she and Mrs Cuthbert are enjoying a right good gossip in the waiting room, so…'

The likelihood of Hildy Wells noticing she'd had to wait longer than she'd expected was remote.

Tracy grinned. 'I'll send Mairi along.'

And I'll take several very deep breaths, Jess decided. After all, Mairi might simply have come in to tell her to stop jamming up her answering machine. But at least she was here. And if she was here, and they were face to face, maybe—just maybe—she might be able to talk her round.

She didn't need to.

'You can arrange for me to have more X-rays and I'll give you a sputum sample,' Mairi declared the minute she sat down. 'That is what you want, isn't it?' she added, her lips curving slightly when Jess stared at her, open-mouthed. 'What all those messages on my answering machine were about?'

'Why, y-yes—th-they were,' Jess stammered. 'I just… I'm delighted, of course—you've no idea how much—but what made you change your mind?'

'Couldn't really do anything else, with that man of yours visiting me every day,' Mairi replied ruefully.

'That man of— You mean, Ezra—Dr Dunbar's been visiting you?' Jess exclaimed.

'Every afternoon for the past week, regular as clockwork. Said he came round because I made the best coffee on the island, but I'm not an idiot.'

So *that* was why Ezra's home visits had been taking so long lately. Much as Jess longed to know how he'd managed to talk Mairi round, she wasn't about to lose the impetus of the moment by asking her. Not yet, at any rate.

'Stay right where you are,' she ordered, grasping her crutches and pulling herself upright. 'I won't be a minute. I just need to get a container from the store cupboard for the sputum sample.'

'There's no hurry!' Mairi called after her, amusement plain in her voice. 'I'm not going anywhere.'

Maybe she wasn't, but Jess wasn't about to take the chance. Not when Mairi was here, and ready, and willing.

'Hey, watch out!' Ezra exclaimed, catching her just in time as she negotiated the entrance to the store cupboard much too fast and sent one of her crutches clattering to the floor. 'Isn't one fractured leg enough for you, or are you trying for a matching pair?'

She shook her head and laughed. 'Ezra, has anyone ever told you you're *wonderful*?'

'Hey, I just happened to be in the right place at the right time.'

'Not *this*, you ninny! Mairi Morrison. She's in my consulting room, and she's agreed to the sputum sample and more X-rays, and it's all because of you!'

He looked embarrassed. 'I didn't do anything—'

'Says the man who's been visiting her every day for the past week on the quiet. Ezra, I'm so pleased I could...' Yikes! She'd almost said 'kiss you'. Get a *grip*, Jess. Get your brain in gear and your mouth under control before you make a complete and utter fool of yourself. 'It's terrific news, isn't it?' she hurried on quickly. 'I've been hoping, praying—'

'Could what?'

'Sorry?' she floundered, hoping he wasn't asking what she thought he might be, but he was.

'You said, "I'm so pleased I could",' he prompted, 'and then you stopped.'

'Did I?' she mumbled.

Think of something Jess, she told herself. Think of something, and make it good. And she probably would have been able to if she hadn't suddenly realised he was still holding her lightly round the waist, and her hands were still resting on his broad, muscular chest.

Lord, but what deep grey eyes he had, and such long eyelashes, too. Completely wasted on a man, of course, her practical side observed, but right now—strangely enough— she wasn't feeling very practical. Not when the most deliciously warm sensations seemed to be uncurling somewhere deep within her.

'I...um...' Her mind was a blank. A complete and utter blank. 'I...I'm afraid I can't remember what I was going to say.'

'Can't you?'

Was it her imagination or did his voice sound deeper, huskier? His heart rate was certainly slightly fast. Hers was jumping around all over the place.

'Crazy, really,' she said, knowing she was babbling but quite unable to stop. 'Not remembering, I mean.'

'So what are you doing out here?' he asked. 'I mean, why aren't you with her?'

'With who?' she said in confusion.

'Mairi Morrison.'

'Because I need…' Oh, hell, what had she needed again? Oh, yes, now she remembered. 'A sterile container for the sputum sample.'

'Ah.'

His reply was almost a sigh, and she shivered. Couldn't help herself. His heart rate *was* too fast. So was hers.

'And then I must phone Bev,' she said, desperately trying to drag her addled brain into some sort of working order, 'to organise—'

'More X-rays.' He nodded. 'But, Jess…'

But what? she wondered, then ceased to care. He was closer. She couldn't for the life of her figure out how when they'd been already standing toe to toe, but he was definitely closer.

Was he going to kiss her? Did she want him to? Stupid question!

Nervously she moistened her lips, saw his pupils dilate as his eyes followed the action, then completely without warning he suddenly released her.

'Right—fine. I'd better not keep you, then,' he muttered, before banging back into his consulting room leaving her staring, open-mouthed, after him.

He'd been going to kiss her—surely he had—so why had he changed his mind? Or maybe he hadn't changed his mind. Maybe… Oh, cripes! Maybe he'd never intended kissing her at all, and she'd just imagined it. In which case she was in trouble. Big trouble.

'Everything OK, Jess?' Tracy smiled as she bounced down the corridor towards her, carrying the box of pharmaceutical supplies which had arrived in the morning's post.

'I— Yes, couldn't be better,' she managed brightly. 'I'm just…'

Oh, hell, her brains were mush again. Mairi Morrison. Mairi Morrison's sputum sample. Concentrate on work, Jess, she told herself, bending to recover the crutch she'd dropped, only to discover her hands were shaking. Pull yourself together, and concentrate on work.

And she managed to do just that. Managed to take Mairi's sample, carefully label it 'For Urgent Attention' and then phone Bev at the hospital to organise more X-rays. It was only when all the practicalities had been completed that she couldn't prevent her mind returning to Ezra. But at least it was work-related, she told herself, purely in the interests of the practice, to ask Mairi how Ezra had managed to achieve what she'd so singularly failed to do.

'You mean, did he talk me into submission?' Mairi declared, her eyes twinkling.

'No—of course not,' Jess floundered, though, in truth, that was exactly what she'd suspected.

'I know what people say,' Mairi nodded. 'That talking to him is like talking to a walking medical dictionary, but we actually only talked about the shadow on my lung on his first visit. The rest of the time we simply chatted about this and that.'

'You did?' Jess said, trying—and failing—to picture Ezra actually chatting to a patient.

'He told me a little bit about his childhood. I might tell you about it some time,' Mairi continued as Jess opened her mouth eagerly, 'but right now all I can say is I trust him. And...' She paused, and looked a little rueful, a little embarrassed. 'I *like* him.'

So did Jess. A lot. But it was all too obviously a one-sided attraction. In two weeks' time he'd leave and her life would go on as it had been before. OK, it might be a little emptier, a little lonelier, but it would go on.

The way to get through the next two weeks was to work, she told herself when Mairi had left with an appointment to see Bev at the Sinclair Memorial that afternoon. If she buried herself in her work she wouldn't have time to think, and thinking, she had decided, was a very bad idea.

Ezra had come to the same conclusion as he sat in his consulting room, only half listening to Mrs Cuthbert's tale of woe about her verruca. If he'd acted on instinct—as every part of his body had urged him to do—he would now know whether Jess's lips were as sweet and soft as they looked instead of still being in a state of unhappy ignorance.

Dammit, she'd looked so appealing, her cheeks flushed, her eyes shining with pleasure because Mairi had finally come into the surgery. Would one tiny little kiss have hurt?

'Yes,' he muttered, and Mrs Cuthbert nodded sagely, her double chin wobbling its agreement.

'That's exactly what I thought, Doctor. The preparations Mr Singh sells in the shop are fine for something small, but if you want your electricity fixed, you don't see someone who can only change a plug, do you? You go to an expert. In fact, as I was saying to my friend, Mrs Wells...'

One little kiss would have been disastrous. Because one little kiss wouldn't have been enough. It would have led to a longer one, a deeper one, and...

'You don't agree, Doctor?' Mrs Cuthbert asked, her plump face creasing into a puzzled frown as he unconsciously shook his head.

With what? he wondered, staring back at her with dismay.

Lord, what in the world was happening to him? He'd had relationships with women in the past, and yet never once had he let his mind wander at work, but in the space of three short weeks with Jess Arden...

'I— Well, of course, there's always two schools of thought, Mrs Cuthbert,' he hedged, praying she might enlighten him, and to his relief, she did.

'Then you think my verruca might benefit from this ointment containing podo—pody...'

'Podophyllum,' he finished for her thankfully. 'Verrucas

certainly seem to respond well to it, but I've got to tell you it's a rather painful way of getting rid of them.'

Mrs Cuthbert sniffed. 'Doctor, as a woman who's had three children—one of them a breech birth—I think I can stand a little pain.'

So could he, Ezra told himself firmly as he wrote her out a prescription. OK, so living with Jess had unexpectedly sent his libido into overdrive. And OK, so it was becoming increasingly difficult for him to sleep at night, knowing that the person who could ease his discomfort was lying just a few feet away from him, but he'd do it. To do anything else would be unforgivable.

But, oh, so very pleasurable, he thought with a sigh when he joined Jess in her consulting room for coffee at the end of morning surgery and couldn't fail to notice how the winter sunshine was illuminating her red curls.

'Something wrong?' he asked, seeing her frown as she read the letter she was holding.

'Not wrong as much as puzzling. According to the infirmary, Robb MacGregor definitely hasn't got a peptic ulcer.'

'Robb MacGregor—he's the builder you initially thought had anaemia, isn't he?'

She nodded. 'The dark stools, the bouts of diarrhoea—everything seemed to point to an ulcer, but now I'm wondering if he could have chronic fatigue syndrome. He's certainly been working very long hours these past six years, trying to establish his business, and I know mental and physical stress can be a contributory factor, but...'

'You're not convinced,' Ezra finished for her, helping himself to one of the chocolate biscuits Tracy had brought in with their coffee.

Jess eyed the biscuits longingly, then gave in to the temptation. Oh, what the hell. She could start her diet next week. Right now she needed some comfort food.

'I still think I've missed something, Ezra.'

'Would you like me to check him over when he comes

in for the results of his test?' he offered. 'I'm not suggesting you haven't been thorough—'

'You can suggest whatever you like, provided you find out what's wrong with him,' she said, and he laughed. A deep, rich, throaty sound which seemed to wrap itself round her heart, warming it.

Oh, how she liked this man. Liked him so much. OK, so he could be over-organising and officious at times and, OK, so she knew nothing about him, but sometimes a girl didn't need to know much about a man. Sometimes a girl just took one look and—

Stop it, she told herself. *Just stop it!* You're sounding like some dopey thirteen-year-old mooning over the high-school heartthrob. You're thirty-two years old, for heaven's sake. Get it into your thick skull that the man's not interested. OK, so you're attracted to him, but you'll get over it. It's like the measles. Uncomfortable while it lasts, but if you're sensible and careful, it leaves no lasting damage.

'Which makes the sixth case of confirmed measles we've had since last week.'

Measles—who had measles, real, honest-to-goodness measles? she wondered in dismay as Ezra added more milk to his coffee. Dammit, what in the world was happening to her? She'd never let her mind wander at work before, and now she didn't have a clue what he was talking about.

'You're…ah…absolutely sure it's measles?' she hazarded, hoping he might give her more information, and to her relief he did.

'Jess, I might never have been a GP, but I think even I can recognise the rash.' He smiled. 'And I can assure you, Robin Clark definitely has measles. A very bad attack, too. He has an infection of the middle ear with quite a severe discharge of pus, so I've started him on antibiotics.'

'How's his chest? He was always a bit bronchial, even when he was a baby.'

'At the moment it's clear, but I've told his mother to

phone us right away if he develops a wheezy cough with phlegm. I also told her—'

Jess never did find out what Ezra had told Robin's mother. The door of her consulting room suddenly opened, and Cath appeared, scarlet-cheeked with embarrassment, with Tracy at her side.

'Jess, what am I going to *do*?' she exclaimed. 'I was *sure* I'd ordered more of the diphtheria, pertussis and tetanus triple vaccine. Tracy said we were low on it, and I remember phoning the rep, quoting the reference number— only I've obviously quoted the *wrong* reference number. And it's my mums and babies group tomorrow, and—'

'What, exactly, has happened, Cath?' Jess interrupted, totally bewildered.

'The order arrived this morning—'

'It was in the box I was carrying when I met you in the corridor, Jess,' Tracy chipped in helpfully.

Jess remembered. She also remembered what had happened shortly before Tracy had appeared, and preferred not to.

'But when Tracy unpacked it…' Tears of mortification welled in Cath's eyes. 'It was full of condoms. Twenty-four dozen packets of *condoms*!'

Tracy smothered a giggle, Jess bit down hard on her lip to prevent herself from joining in, and it was left to Ezra to say, 'Look on the bright side, Cath. If there's an all-night rave in the village hall this weekend, at least we're not going to run out.'

'It's *not* funny, Ezra!' the receptionist protested. 'I've been hammering away at my mums and babies group for the last six months, trying to convince them of the benefits of immunisation, and now—when I've actually got eight of them to agree—I can't vaccinate more than two of them!'

'Have you tried faxing the company, asking them to send the vaccine by special delivery?' Jess suggested.

'They can't guarantee it will arrive for tomorrow,' Cath exclaimed. 'Not with us living on an island.'

So there was nothing they could do. Nothing but hope that if the vaccine didn't turn up in time the mums would be prepared to wait.

'Do you think I should go after her?' Ezra murmured in a concerned undertone as Cath disappeared back out the door. 'Maybe that joke wasn't very helpful…'

'You were only trying to make her laugh,' Jess said reassuringly, 'and I'm sure she'll understand once she calms down. The trouble is, everything seems to be getting on top of her lately.'

He nodded. 'I've noticed.'

And me giving her an earful earlier probably didn't help, Jess thought guiltily. Well, she'd simply have to apologise. Again. In fact, now she came to think of it, the only member of staff she hadn't managed to hurt or offend over the last three weeks was Tracy, and she had a horrible feeling it was only a matter of time.

Actually, probably a very short time, she realised irritably, seeing the girl flutter her eyelashes at Ezra when she handed him his list of home visits.

'He's terrific, isn't he?' Tracy sighed the minute Ezra had gone. 'So dark, so tall, so masterful.'

Jess thought so, too, but never would she have admitted it.

'I thought you and Danny were dating?' she said instead, hoping she sounded more casual than she felt.

'Not any more. Danny…' Tracy waved her hand dismissively. 'He's just a boy, whereas Ezra's a man, if you know what I mean.'

Jess rather thought she did. Just as she also now understood why Danny had taken to hanging around the surgery, looking distinctly woebegone.

Not that Ezra had ever given Tracy any encouragement. In fact, Jess strongly suspected he regarded their junior receptionist as simply a bubbly, bouncy, slightly scatty teenager, but teenagers' hearts could be broken. So could a thirty-two-year-old woman's, if she was stupid and lonely.

And that, she decided, as she began ploughing through her paperwork, was what was wrong with her. She was lonely. For the last three years she'd had no social life—had never found time to fit one in—so when the burden of her work was lessened who was she most likely to become attracted to? A man she saw every day.

Her conviction that she'd finally discovered the answer to the disturbing feelings which kept plaguing her lasted for the rest of the afternoon. Remained firmly in place even when Ezra drove her home. And then completely fell apart when he suddenly smiled at her halfway through dinner and her heart flipped over in a depressingly familiar fashion.

So much for it simply being loneliness and proximity, she thought with a deep sigh when she went to bed. So much for there being a totally rational explanation. When it came right down to it, she was as silly as Tracy.

Well, it was stopping right now, she told herself. No more wimpy, pathetic Jess Arden. Welcome back, the old tough Jess Arden who would never have allowed herself to be distracted and confused by a pair of deep grey eyes and a slightly crooked smile.

And on that positive note she fell asleep, only to wake less than three hours later to find Ezra standing by her bed.

'What is it—what's wrong?' she asked, her bleary eyes taking in his obviously hastily thrown-on sweater and denims.

'Denise Fullarton's bleeding. I'd go myself but she's specifically asked for you.'

Jess's heart plummeted to the pit of her stomach. Denise was ten weeks pregnant, and she was bleeding, which probably meant she was losing her baby. Her fourth baby.

'Can you manage?' Ezra continued, seeing her wince as she levered herself upright.

She couldn't, not with the speed she knew was necessary at a time like this, but...

'Jess.' He both sounded and looked impatient. 'We have

to hurry. Can you get up and dressed quickly by yourself, or not?'

She bit her lip, hating to ask him for help, but knowing there was no alternative. 'Not really, no.'

'OK, what clothes do you need?'

'Bra, knickers, sweater and skirt. I can get the bra and sweater on by myself,' she continued, watching him as he hurried to her chest of drawers, 'and if you bring me the brown skirt with the buttons down the front I can manage that, but...' Her cheeks flamed with colour, and she swallowed hard. Get it over with, Jess, she told herself. You're the old, tough Jess, remember. Tell him what you need him to do, and get it over with. 'It's...it's my knickers. I can't bend my leg, you see—'

'You want me to put on your knickers?' he interrupted faintly.

'N-not a-all the way up,' she stammered, wishing she could see his face, but he was still rummaging through her chest of drawers. Actually, no, he wasn't. He'd stopped, but he hadn't turned round. 'I just— If you could just slip them up over my knees a little bit, I'll be able to pull them up the rest of the way myself.'

He muttered something, but she couldn't make out what it was.

'Ezra—'

'Knickers, bra, sweater, skirt.' He slammed the chest of drawers shut. 'Right. No problem. Got them.'

And I want to be anywhere but here, Jess thought when he came back to the bed and knelt down in front of her.

You can do this, she told herself as he lifted one of her feet and slipped it through her knickers. Just think of something else and pretend it isn't really happening to you.

But how to think of something else when the baggy T-shirt she normally wore to bed kept riding up despite her best efforts to prevent it? How to ignore the gentle touch of his fingers against her bare skin as he slipped her knickers slowly upwards, sending shivers of sensation through

her entire body, tightening her chest wall? And how—
how—to pretend his dark head wasn't almost resting in her
lap and his hands weren't inching closer and closer to an
area of her body which she normally barely registered and
yet now was all too acutely and devastatingly aware of?

'Is…is that far enough, or do you need me to pull them
higher?'

His voice sounded slightly choked, constricted, and she
knew without looking that his gaze was fixed firmly on her
duvet cover as though pink roses in wicker baskets were
the most riveting sight in the world.

'I can manage now, thank you,' she replied in a rush,
her own eyes fixed desperately on the wall opposite.

'Right. I…I'll get the car started while you put on the
rest of your clothes,' he muttered, and before she could
answer he was gone.

Not that she could have said anything if she'd tried.

Lord, she'd never been so embarrassed in her whole life.
Embarrassed, and vulnerable, and exposed. And to be fair
to Ezra, he'd got her knickers on as quickly as he could.
No deliberate fumbling, no smart remarks. Many men in
his position would have taken advantage of the situation,
but he hadn't. Not even a little bit, she thought wistfully.

Oh, get a grip, Jess, she told herself, pulling on her
sweater, then angrily buttoning up her skirt. You should be
relieved he didn't take advantage. You should be thanking
your lucky stars he's a gentleman.

And she was—sort of—but…

But nothing, she decided, reaching for her crutches.
Right now Denise is your main priority, not your own ad-
olescent fantasies. Denise needs you, and so does her husband.

Alec Fullarton clearly did need her by the time Ezra had
driven them down to Inverlairg.

'Oh, Jess, thank God you're here!' he exclaimed, his face
chalk white with distress and fear. 'When she started to
bleed, I thought, if she starts crying I can cope with that.

Even if she goes hysterical like she did the last time—well, I'll have to deal with it—but she's just lying there, not saying anything, and it's scaring the hell out of me!'

'Is she bleeding badly, Alec?' Jess asked, following him down the corridor as quickly as she could.

'Not as much as she did the last time.'

'And the blood—is it bright red, or dark in colour? I know you don't want to think about it,' she continued, seeing a flash of pain and anger cross his face, 'but it's important.'

'I know. It's just…' He shook his head. 'It's sort of dark-ish in colour—definitely not bright red.'

Jess glanced across at Ezra. That sounded hopeful. If the bleeding wasn't severe, or the tell-tale bright red which usually signalled that the uterus was beginning to expel the foetus, Denise might not actually be miscarrying.

Denise clearly believed she was.

'It's happening again, isn't it?' she said, her voice flat, devoid of all emotion. 'I'm losing another baby, aren't I?'

'I think you should let us be the best judge of that, don't you?' Jess said gently. 'How's your back—any pain there?'

Denise shook her head.

'No sign of any blood clots either,' Ezra murmured when he pulled back Denise's bedclothes and crouched down beside her.

'What about the cervix?' Jess asked, wishing she could get down beside him but knowing she'd undoubtedly fall over if she tried to.

'Still closed.'

Better and better. If the cervix had started to dilate, a miscarriage was inevitable, but if it stayed shut…

Ezra replaced the bedclothes and stood up. 'Mrs Fullarton, I don't think you're miscarrying. The bleeding seems to have stopped—'

'Because I'm not pregnant any more, that's why,' she interrupted. 'Jess, tell him he doesn't need to lie to me. I've been this way far too many times.'

Jess didn't get the chance to say anything. Ezra took Denise's hand in his and forced her to look up at him.

'Mrs Fullarton—Denise—I'm not lying. If you want, I can call out the air ambulance to have you taken to the mainland for an ultrasound to confirm you're still pregnant, but frankly I don't see the necessity.'

'But the bleeding,' she protested. 'Surely that means I've lost the baby?'

He shook his head. 'Bleeding during pregnancy doesn't always indicate a miscarriage. You could have cervical erosion, or simply a low placental implantation.' He smiled as Denise gazed up at him uncertainly, a warm, gentle smile of encouragement and reassurance. 'A cervical erosion simply means your cervix is more fragile than most women's, and a low placental implantation is doctor-speak for your baby being situated rather low in your tummy.'

'Then...then you think I'm still pregnant?' Denise whispered, her bottom lip suddenly starting to tremble.

'I *know* you're still pregnant,' he declared.

He was learning, Jess thought, watching him. Three weeks ago—even one week—he would have bewildered Denise with medical fact and jargon. Now he was relying solely on her trust in him, and it was working.

'Do you think she might actually manage to carry the baby to full term this time?' she asked when they eventually drove away from the Fullartons', leaving Denise with strict instructions to remain in bed until further notice.

'Her track record's abysmal, but miracles do happen. If we can just get her past the next two weeks and get a stitch in her cervix to keep it closed, we could then start giving her uterine relaxants to keep the pressure off her cervix. Then she might just make it.'

'*Might* being the operative word,' Jess sighed, staring gloomily out into the darkness.

'Hey, what's happened to my little optimist?'

She glanced round to see he was smiling at her and, try

as she might, she couldn't stop her own lips curving in response.

Oh, damn. Damn, damn and triple damn.

This had to stop. It really, *really* had to stop. The way her heart kept skipping a beat, the way she felt all warm, and expectant, and tingly—it was stupid, ridiculous. People walked away from unhappy love affairs and marriages all the time. Well, she couldn't walk away. Not yet, when she needed Ezra's help with the practice. But she sure as heck could start distancing herself. Quite how, she wasn't exactly sure, but there had to be a way. There *must*!

CHAPTER SIX

THERE was, and it was so easy Jess wondered why she'd never thought of it before. All she had to do to prevent those stomach-churning moments was to avoid eye contact. No eye contact, no leapfrogging heart. No eye contact, no peculiar sensations. And it was working, too. Since Denise's threatened miscarriage three days ago she hadn't had one uncomfortable moment.

It was all a question of strategy. Of pinpointing potentially tricky moments and taking evasive action.

Like the coffee-break she shared with Ezra after morning surgery. If she aimed her comments at his left ear, it worked a treat. Being alone with him at home was more difficult, but waiting until the last possible moment to have breakfast had proved a winner. And as for dinner—well, she could always use her leg as an excuse to go to bed early.

Not that she needed an excuse, Jess thought ruefully, uncomfortably shifting her weight as she bent over Grace Henderson to take her blood pressure. Her leg still hurt. Not as much as when she'd fractured it three weeks ago, but enough for her to look forward to crawling into bed at the end of the day.

'How much longer are you going to be in plaster, dear?' Grace asked, watching her with considerable sympathy.

'Some weeks yet, I'm afraid,' Jess murmured, listening intently to the steady flow of Grace's blood.

'It's amazing, how one little accident can turn your life upside down, isn't it?'

Especially if that accident was caused by a man like Ezra Dunbar, Jess thought with an inward sigh.

'I'm so pleased Mairi eventually came to see you,' Grace

continued. 'Normally I don't hold with snooping on your neighbours—live and let live has always been my motto—but I could see she wasn't right.'

'I'm sure Mairi doesn't think you were snooping,' Jess said reassuringly.

'She said she didn't.' Mrs Henderson nodded. 'She also seems to have taken a real shine to your Dr Dunbar—always singing his praises, she is.'

'That's nice,' Jess said noncommittally.

'Will she have to wait long for the results of her tests? She told me she's not worried about them, but…well, it's only human nature to worry, isn't it, dear?'

'It is, and I'm sure they'll be back soon.' In fact, Jess had expected them the previous day. Usually when she put an 'Urgent' sticker on samples the infirmary lab was quick to respond, but this time… 'Your blood pressure's fine, Grace. Exactly the same as last month.'

Grace beamed with relief. 'Thank goodness for that. I certainly don't want another unscheduled trip to the mainland.'

Jess didn't want one either, especially at this time of year. They had been lucky so far this winter—only a few sharp frosts and a little sleet—but it was only the beginning of February and the last thing she wanted was an emergency and no way of getting the patient to the mainland.

'Do you need more of your angina pills, Grace?'

'You'd better give me a repeat prescription, dear. I don't want to run out.'

Neither did Jess, not now she'd sussed out the situation with Ezra. She felt decidedly chirpy when she accompanied Grace back to Reception and saw Will Grant deep in conversation with Tracy.

'What brings you down into town, Will?' She smiled, hearing the anaesthetist laugh at something her junior receptionist had said. 'Bev giving you grief, or are you touting for business?'

'Hoping to raise money, more like.' He smiled back. 'I wondered if you could sell some raffle tickets for us?'

'Sure thing.' Jess nodded. 'Leave them with Tracy, and Cath will find a prominent space for them in the waiting room. What's the raffle for?'

'A new defibrillator for the lifeboat service. Their old one badly needs replacing.'

'I wish we could hold a raffle for a resident surgeon,' Jess sighed, reaching for her next patient's file, and Will laughed.

'I'll suggest it at the next Friends of the Hospital meeting, shall I? Which reminds me,' he continued, 'Bev said she'd really like to talk to you about Mairi Morrison's report. The one she sent over yesterday?'

Jess put down the file she was holding. 'I haven't received—'

'Well, hello there, stranger.' Will beamed, seeing Ezra's dark head appear round the waiting-room door. 'How's the hectic life of an island GP suiting you?'

'Fine, thank you,' Ezra murmured, his eyes following Jess as she headed for Cath's office, a decided frown on her forehead.

'I heard about the operation you did on Simon Ralston's hand. Nifty piece of work by all accounts.'

'It was a pretty standard procedure—'

'Not in our neck of the woods, it's not,' Will declared, clearly intent on praise whether Ezra wanted to hear it or not. Which he didn't. 'In fact, if you hadn't been here the poor bloke would have needed to go to the mainland.'

'Which is a ridiculous state of affairs,' Ezra said, eagerly seizing on Will's observation in the hope of changing the conversation. 'The Sinclair Memorial should have a resident surgeon.'

'Couldn't agree with you more,' Will said, 'but the way things are going, we'll probably not even have a hospital by the end of the year.'

Ezra's eyebrows rose. 'How so?'

'Because, though we have an operating theatre with facilities second to none due to the generosity of the local
population, one day soon somebody in authority is going
to take a really good look at the patients Jess has been
operating on, realise how minor the conditions are and
close us down.'

'But—'

'I know.' Will smiled grimly. 'We're in a catch-22 situation. We can't do big operations because we haven't got
a resident surgeon, and we can't get a resident surgeon
because the operations we're performing are too small to
warrant one.'

'Have you tried advertising?' Ezra suggested. 'I'm sure
there must be a surgeon somewhere, wanting to escape the
rat race.'

'Even if there was, I doubt if he—or she—would be
prepared to come to Greensay. Most of the work at the
hospital is pretty routine, you see, which wouldn't appeal
to a top-notch surgeon. What we really need is a good all-
rounder who would also be prepared to help Jess by working part time with her.'

Ezra nodded, only to suddenly realise that Will was gazing at him expectantly. 'Don't look at me. I'm not looking
for a job.'

'But you'd be perfect.'

'And I'm not interested,' Ezra said firmly. 'The arrangement I made with Jess is purely temporary.'

'I don't suppose there's any chance you might change—
OK, enough said.' Will sighed, seeing Ezra's eyebrows
snap down. 'You're not interested. Got the message.'

Ezra sighed, too, as he watched Will leave the health
centre. The man meant well but how to explain to him that
he was also in a catch-22 situation? That there was no way
he could ever set foot in an operating theatre again, and
even if he could, he most certainly wouldn't be applying
for a post as part-time surgeon at the Sinclair Memorial
Hospital.

Not even for Jess? his mind whispered, and he groaned inwardly.

Lord, but he still didn't know how he'd managed to keep his hands off her that night. Kneeling in front of her, all too aware of the outline of her full breasts through her T-shirt, the hard nubs of her nipples. And those damn knickers. They'd kept catching on her plaster cast, and he'd kept trying to pull them up, and she'd kept trying to hold onto the hem of her T-shirt so he couldn't see, and he *had* seen, so that by the time he'd finished he didn't know who was trembling most—him or Jess.

Jess must have sensed his inner turmoil because she'd been distinctly cool and distant towards him these past few days. Which was good. Creating a barrier between them was good, because the last thing he wanted was an affair with her.

He snorted briefly. Hell, who was he trying to kid? Of course he did. He wanted to make love to her—badly—but Jess deserved better than him. A man with no job, no future.

'Are you ready for Mr Guthrie now, Dr Dunbar?' Tracy asked.

He wasn't, but he took the file she was holding out to him and pasted a smile to his lips as the man Mairi Morrison considered ideal husband material for Jess limped slowly towards him.

'Your foot doesn't seem to be getting any better, Mr Guthrie,' he observed, ushering him towards his consulting room.

'That's because it's not,' the portly farmer grumbled. 'In fact, these last few nights I don't think I've had a wink of sleep, and it's really getting to me.'

Tell me about it, Ezra thought ruefully as Brian slipped off his shoe and sock. He hadn't been getting much sleep recently either, and even less since a certain red-headed doctor had asked him to help her with her knickers.

'I think it looks worse, Doctor.'

So did Ezra as he stared down at Brian's foot with dismay. 'Have you been keeping to the diet sheet I gave you—taking the pills I prescribed?'

'Of course,' Brian Guthrie protested.

'You've not knocked your foot—dropped something on it?'

'Doctor, if I'd knocked this foot, you'd have heard my scream down in Inverlairg.'

Ezra's frown deepened, then a sudden thought flashed into his mind. 'You haven't been taking aspirin, have you?'

Brian Guthrie's plump cheeks reddened slightly. 'Just the odd one—now and again. I've been doing a lot of paperwork recently, you see, and that always gives me a headache.'

'And I told you that you mustn't take *any* aspirin,' Ezra reminded him. 'It lessens your kidneys' ability to filter out uric acid, and that's why your gout is worse.'

Brian looked distinctly belligerent. 'Doctor, if I get a bad headache I've no intention of suffering it when a couple of aspirin will help.'

'Even if that means you'll eventually develop chronic gout?' Ezra demanded.

'I don't see how much more chronic it can get,' the farmer muttered. 'It's bloody sore enough as it is.'

'Oh, it can get a lot worse than this, believe me,' Ezra said. 'If you don't get your gout under control, crystals of uric salts will settle in your joints, leading to a condition very similar to osteoarthritis with all its crippling effects. And then you'll undoubtedly develop kidney stones, not to mention doing permanent damage to your kidneys.'

Brian gulped. 'It's…it's that serious?'

Ezra nodded. 'It's that serious. No aspirin under any circumstances, Mr Guthrie, OK?' He reached for his prescription pad. 'I'll give you something you can take for your headaches, but even that must only be taken in moderation.'

Brian sat in silence while Ezra wrote out the prescription,

but when he handed it to him he cleared his throat awk-wardly.

'I was wondering, Doctor—not that I've any complaints about your treatment so, please, don't think so—but Jess—Dr Arden—she's normally my doctor, and I was wondering when I might become her patient again?'

Ezra snapped Brian Guthrie's file shut. 'I really couldn't say. Dr Arden will be in plaster for quite some time yet, and when her locum arrives—'

'She's getting another locum?' The farmer's surprise was clear. 'But I thought—assumed—you'd be staying on until she was fit again?'

'I'm afraid not, and when the locum arrives it will be up to Dr Arden to allocate her patients.'

Brian digested this information, then to Ezra's dismay looked suddenly almost coy. 'The thing is, I'm very fond of Jess.' Quickly Ezra got to his feet, not wanting to hear any more, but Brian didn't take the hint. 'I—well, not to beat about the bush, Dr Dunbar—I'm hoping she and I might get married one day.'

The words 'over my dead body' sprang to Ezra's lips, and he bit them back with an effort. It was none of his business if Jess married Brian Guthrie. Nothing she did, or how she chose to live her life, was any of his business. So why did the thought of her in Brian Guthrie's arms make him want to hit something—someone?

Because he was going crazy, he decided as he accompanied the farmer back to the waiting room. A few weeks on Greensay and he'd gone from a man who'd always abhorred physical violence to a man who would now—if he'd given in to his instincts—be under arrest on two charges of grievous bodily harm.

And something had obviously got under Jess's skin, too, judging by the sound of angry, raised voices coming from Cath's office.

'Cath seems to have lost something important,' Tracy whispered breathlessly, her eyes sparkling with keen interest. 'A report—or a letter—from Bev Grant. I can't make out what they're saying—'

She didn't need to. Cath's office door was suddenly thrown open and Jess appeared, her green eyes blazing.

'What is it—what's wrong?' Ezra asked, seeing Cath shoot off in the direction of the toilets, her cheeks red and tearstained.

'Not here,' Jess replied tightly. 'In my consulting room.'

He followed her silently, but the minute her door was safely closed he couldn't help but say, 'Jess, I don't know what's happened, but bawling out Cath—'

'Look at the dates on these!' she interrupted, thrusting two letters into his hands. He glanced down at them, then up at her, and she nodded. 'Yesterday. Mairi Morrison's sputum results came back from the lab yesterday, and so did Bev Grant's report on her X-rays. Cath says they must have got lost amongst all the bumph which comes into the health centre but, dammit, she's my senior receptionist and practice nurse. It's her *business* not to lose things!'

'I agree,' he said, 'but don't you think you might have gone a little bit over—?'

'Read them, Ezra,' she demanded. 'Read what's wrong with Mairi.'

He stared back at her for a second, then sat down and obediently began to read them. He read them through once, then he read through them again, and when he eventually looked up at her, shock and amazement were plain on his face.

'Mairi's got *TB*? But—'

'I know.' Jess nodded. 'It's a disease you normally associate with the end of the nineteenth century, not with the twenty-first. And did you notice that the sputum sample showed up as thin red rods after the application of the Ziehl-Nielsen stain? It means she hasn't simply got TB, she's also highly infectious.'

'Jess…Jess, that means we're going to have to do tuberculin tests on everyone on the island!' Ezra exclaimed.

'*Now* do you see why I was so angry?' she declared. 'Every hour is vital in a case like this.'

He stared down at the letters in his hand, and a slight frown creased his forehead. 'I can see the need for haste, Jess, but I think you should apologise to Cath. OK, so she was in the wrong—'

'And not for the first time,' she interrupted. 'There was that fiasco over the condoms—'

'And you told me yourself she's under a lot of pressure at the moment,' he pointed out. 'Look, she's probably feeling pretty wretched right now, and we really need her with us on this. She's a fully qualified nurse and three people can test for the presence of TB faster than two.'

She bit her lip. He was right, on both counts. She shouldn't have lost her temper but she'd been so worried about Mairi, and when she'd discovered what was wrong with her... A surge of panic welled up inside her. 'Ezra, how are we going to cope? There's over six hundred people on Greensay, and to screen them all quickly—'

'We'll tackle them one day at a time.'

'But you'll be leaving soon.'

'Do you think I'd run out on you at a time like this?' he protested. 'I'm going nowhere—not even when your locum arrives—until we've tested everyone on the island.'

It was what she'd hoped—prayed—he might say, but to hear him actually say it... A prickle of tears clogged her throat. 'I...I don't know what to say.'

'How about "Yes, please" and "Thank you, Ezra"?' He smiled.

It was what he'd said to her once before. Heavens, was it only three weeks ago? It seemed like a lifetime. As though she'd known him a lifetime. But before she could say anything his face suddenly grew serious.

'Jess, you'll have to get Mairi down here fast—this afternoon if possible. Get her down here, give her the results of her tests and get her started on her treatment immediately. Once we start sending out screening invitations there's bound to be a certain amount of public panic, and the last thing we want is Mairi turning into a social leper.'

He was right but, after finding Cath, apologising to her and asking her to phone Mairi, never had a morning surgery seemed both so long and yet too short.

She diagnosed yet another case of measles, bringing the latest total to ten, treated Mrs Wilson for a bad case of thrush and confirmed that Sybil Martin's youngest most definitely had croup. But always at the back of her mind was how she was going to break the news to Mairi.

The woman thought she had lung cancer, and for her now to learn she had TB and was a real health risk to the people of Greensay... It was a consultation she didn't want to have.

'But I can't have TB!' Mairi exclaimed, staring across at her in disbelief. 'Jess, you've known me since you were a little girl. I've scarcely had a cold or a day's illness in my life!'

'Did anyone in your family ever have TB, Mairi?'

'One of my aunts did, but she died over forty years ago, and it's not the sort of thing you can have for forty years and not know about, is it?'

'Well, actually, yes, you can. Look, let me try to explain,' Jess said as Mairi looked even more confused. 'Most people growing up in Britain in the past would—like you— have come into contact with someone with tuberculosis. If the person they came into contact with coughed a lot then it's likely they inhaled a small amount of the bacteria into their own lungs. It wouldn't have been enough to give them tuberculosis, but it would have been enough to give them an infection that we call primary TB, which actually helped to build up a partial immunity to the disease.'

Mairi frowned. 'You mean sort of like when you get a vaccination against smallpox or measles, and they actually give you a small dose of the disease?'

'Rather like that, yes.'

'But if I was immune to it before, why have I got tuberculosis now?' Mairi demanded.

Jess sighed. 'I'm afraid that's the million-dollar question. Occasionally—and we don't yet know why—the immunity to the original infection becomes weaker and the TB bacteria break out of their original site and go on to develop into full-blown tuberculosis.'

'And that's what I've got now?' Mairi asked.

Jess nodded. 'That's what you've got now.'

Blind panic appeared in Mairi's eyes as she took this in. 'Jess, my aunt had to go into a special isolation hospital on the mainland, and she was there for *years*!'

'Things are very different now, Mairi,' Jess said quickly. 'In fact, with modern treatment, we can actually stop the progress of TB within a few days of starting treatment, although a complete cure usually takes a bit longer.'

Actually, quite a lot longer, but she saw no need to tell Mairi that. Not when she knew how devastated Mairi was going to be when told that the entire community would have to be screened because she was highly infectious.

'Ezra, it was awful, really awful,' Jess said miserably when he returned from his home visits and drove her into town to do their weekly shop. 'All she kept saying over and over again was that she'd put the lives of the island children at risk, and nothing I said made any difference.'

'Jess—'

'I couldn't even get her to go home,' she continued, as though he hadn't spoken. 'She insisted on being taken into the Sinclair Memorial despite me saying there was no need—'

'Jess, forget it—at least for the rest of the day,' he said gently. 'You've started her treatment and she'll eventually recover, so there's nothing else you can do for her at the moment. You're going to need all your strength once we start sending out screening letters tomorrow, so make the most of the fact you've no surgery tonight and try to relax.'

He was right, of course, and she tried—really tried—to do as he suggested, showing an interest in the food he bought, the meals he was planning for the week ahead, but it was a relief when he suggested she wait by the car while he and Nazir packed all their groceries into carrier bags.

How many tuberculin tests could they reasonably do in a day? One every ten minutes—one every five? But they'd have normal surgeries as well, plus home visits, and then they'd have to wait for the results from the mainland. Thank God for Ezra. If he hadn't agreed to help, she didn't know what she would have done.

'Excuse me, miss?'

Jess turned with a slight frown to see a young man in his mid-twenties gazing at her uncertainly.

'The man you were just talking to in the shop,' he continued. 'You wouldn't happen to know if his name is Ezra Dunbar, would you?' She nodded, and his eyes lit up. 'I *thought* it was him, but the beard—it completely threw me. Does he live here now, do you know?'

'For the moment, he does,' she replied. 'I'm Jess Arden, by the way, the local GP.'

'Ah,' the young man said as though that somehow explained everything. 'How is he?'

'Why don't you ask him yourself?' Jess smiled. 'He's just collecting some groceries from the shop but he won't be more than a couple of minutes.'

'I wouldn't want to impose…'

'You'd hardly be doing that if you're a friend of his,' Jess pointed out. 'In fact, I'm sure he'd be delighted to see you.'

'I wouldn't exactly call us friends,' the young man admitted, 'but I worked for him at the Royal in London, and I always wondered—well, we all did—what happened to him—where he'd gone to—after he left the hospital.' He shook his head in apparent disbelief. 'Wait until I tell everyone—they'll never believe it. Talk about coincidence—'

'You said Dr Dunbar worked at the Royal in London?' Jess interrupted, all thoughts of tuberculin tests temporarily forgotten.

'He was one of its major stars. Youngest ever heart surgeon at twenty-seven, head of his own unit at thirty-three. The man was a living legend.'

Jess could believe it. His suturing of Simon Ralston's hand hadn't simply been good, it had been brilliant.

'And then a year ago…' The young man sighed. 'Well, as you can imagine, we were all thunderstruck when he resigned. It was tragic, really—all that talent and ability— to end like that. Mind you, he really couldn't have done anything else under the circumstances.'

Jess's ears pricked up. 'The circumstances?' she prompted.

'Mind you, I have to say there weren't a lot of tears shed when he went,' the young man continued. 'He didn't exactly endear himself to the staff at the Royal, you see. Too abrasive by half.'

Jess could well believe that, but she wasn't interested in hearing how abrasive Ezra had been. 'You said Ezra left the Royal a year ago…'

'I think that's everything, Jess,' Ezra said, appearing by her side without warning.

Not yet it wasn't, she thought determinedly. Not when she was so close to finally getting an answer to the one question Ezra would never answer.

'Ezra, this gentleman—'

'I'm sorry, I never did introduce myself, did I?' The young man laughed. 'Trevor Taylor—Dr Trevor Taylor. It's good to see you again, sir,' he continued, turning to Ezra.

Ezra didn't look as though he shared Trevor Taylor's pleasure. In fact, he looked furious and Jess wasn't surprised when the young doctor eventually made a very hasty retreat after a few tortuous and decidedly uncomfortable pleasantries.

'You weren't very polite,' she observed as Ezra yanked open the boot of his car with quite unnecessary force.

'Wasn't I?' he replied tersely.

'Dr Taylor said he was a colleague of yours, that he'd worked with you at the Royal in London.'

Their groceries were stowed with scant regard to any of the breakable items and the boot lid was slammed shut. 'I can't say I remember him.'

'Well, he remembers you,' Jess said, refusing to give up. 'A living legend, he said. So talented, and gifted, he said, and how tragic it was when you resigned, but you couldn't really have done anything else in the circumstances.'

He stared back at her silently, then yanked open the passenger door. 'Our vegetables and meat are defrosting. Unless you want to eat the lot tonight, or risk salmonella by re-freezing them, I suggest we go home, don't you?'

And that was obviously the end of the matter as far as he was concerned, but it wasn't finished for her. Not by a long shot, she decided as he drove them home. She had no intention of leaving it, not after what Trevor Taylor had said.

Tragic was the word he'd used to describe Ezra's resignation. Did he mean he'd had an affair with a colleague's wife, and had been forced to resign because of it? Unconsciously she shook her head. People didn't resign over affairs nowadays, and Ezra didn't seem to her to be the kind of man who'd throw in a job because he was nursing a broken heart.

Not that she actually knew him, of course, she realised, glancing surreptitiously across at him. Lord, but he still looked furious. Furious, white-lipped, and...and ill.

He definitely looked ill, she thought with concern, seeing the way his hands were clenched on the steering-wheel, the tiny beads of sweat on his forehead. He'd looked like this the night he'd taken her to the Sinclair Memorial. And when the tray of coffee-cups had suddenly slipped through his fingers for no apparent reason.

Oh, dear God, was *that* why Trevor Taylor had said Ezra's resignation had been tragic—because he was ill? So ill he couldn't work any more? So ill he might... might...even be dying?

It made sense—horrible, awful sense—and Jess waited only until he'd carried their groceries into her cottage before she grasped him urgently by the arm. 'Ezra, what Dr Taylor said—'

'You just can't leave it alone, can you?' he exclaimed furiously. 'You have to keep on picking and picking at it like a scab! OK, I'll tell you why I resigned. I resigned because I almost killed the last person I operated on!'

'You mean you had unexpected complications—'

'No, I don't mean I had unexpected complications!' he retorted. 'They say pride comes before a fall, and they're right. I was demonstrating a new surgical technique I'd perfected to a group of students,' he continued as she stared at him in confusion, 'and I got so caught up in their admiration and awe that I missed something even a third-year med student would have noticed, and if one of my colleagues hadn't realised it in time my patient would have died.'

She couldn't disguise her relief. 'Is that all?'

'All—*all*!' he spat out, and she coloured.

'I thought you were ill, Ezra. I thought maybe you had a tumour. I thought...I thought you might be *dying*.'

'Sometimes I wish I was,' he muttered so quietly she hardly heard him, but she did.

'Ezra, there's not a doctor living who hasn't made a mistake,' she said quickly, hating to see him like this, so drawn and stricken. 'We're not gods, remember, and at least someone noticed your mistake—'

'But I can't operate any more, Jess,' he flared. 'My nerve's gone. The minute I hit an operating theatre I get the shakes, feel sick. Damn it, I can't even lift a scalpel without my hands trembling!'

'But—'

'Jess, there *is* no Ezra Dunbar without my skill!' He thrust his hands in front of her face. 'These are—were—my tools. With them I could transform people's lives. With them I could make people whole again. Without them...' his face twisted bitterly '...I'm nothing.'

'You're wrong—so wrong,' she cried. 'Yes, your skill was a part of you—OK, so it was a large part,' she continued quickly as he turned from her in exasperation, 'but there's more to you than that.'

He didn't believe her. She could see it in his eyes as he began dragging their shopping out of the carrier bags and slamming it on the kitchen table, and she hopped awkwardly round the table towards him.

'Ezra, listen to me. Scientists are already making machines which can do minor operations. In twenty—maybe thirty—years they'll probably be able to build machines which can perform major heart and brain surgery, but do you think people will ever praise these machines—raise statues to them? Do you think anyone will ever grieve, feel their life is over, when that machine breaks down and can't be mended?'

He shook his head. 'You don't understand—'

'It's *you* who doesn't understand,' she insisted. 'Ezra, you're not a machine, you're a person, and it's that person, what you were like—how much joy, or peace, or happiness you brought into other people's lives—that people will remember.'

His lip curled. 'And what little book of feel-good quotations did that come out of?'

A deep wash of colour spread across her cheeks. 'Look, if you honestly don't think you'll ever be able to operate again, you could teach. Teach the skills you have to others. Or...or, if you don't want to do that,' she continued, seeing the look of derision he threw her, 'I think you could make a very good GP. I've seen you with my patients. OK, so maybe at first you were a little formal—a little jargon-obsessed—but that's only because you weren't used to talk-

ing to patients. If you can't operate any more, you could
be a GP.'

'And spend the rest of my life dishing out pills and advice to people with piles and verrucas?' He shook his head
with distaste. 'No way!'

Jess stared at him silently, her sympathy giving way to
anger. He'd said it had been his pride which had caused
his downfall, but he hadn't learned anything from the experience. He was still proud—proud and arrogant—and
how she'd ever been attracted to him she couldn't imagine.
Right now, she didn't even *like* him.

'So, it's your ego that's hurt more than anything else, is
it?' she said, ice-cold. 'Now you can't be the big cheese,
the high-flying general, you don't want to slum it with the
common foot soldiers.'

'You don't understand—'

'Too damn right I don't,' she retorted. 'But, then, I'm
only an ordinary, run-of-the-mill GP. There's nothing special about me, nothing unique. I'm not a big-shot surgeon
with an ego to match.'

'Jess—'

'You've still got two arms, two legs and a brain that
functions, Ezra. There's a hell of a lot of people out there
who are considerably worse off than you, so stop wallow-
ing in self-pity and get a life!'

'Now, just a minute—'

'And as for your offer to stay on after my locum arrives
to help me with the tuberculosis screening—don't bother!'
she continued for good measure. 'I wouldn't want you to
demean yourself by working with the common herd!'

And before he could reply she'd grasped her crutches
and hopped out of the kitchen, leaving him staring, open-
mouthed, after her.

CHAPTER SEVEN

'WELL, of course I was deeply shocked when I heard about Mairi Morrison,' Wattie Hope declared, looking anything but. 'Tuberculosis is something I never expected to hear about again in my lifetime and, knowing how infectious it is, I thought I'd better come down pretty smart and get this test thing done.'

You and half the island, Jess thought wearily as she reached for her box of tuberculin.

Quite how the news of Mairi's TB had spread so fast was beyond her. Two days—that was all it had taken for her condition to become common knowledge—and, as Ezra had predicted, immediate panic had been the result.

Nobody was prepared to wait for a screening appointment. Everyone wanted a test, and they wanted one now. Cath and Tracy were doing their level best to ensure surgeries were kept solely for people requiring consultations, but they were fighting a losing battle and people who really needed to see a doctor were constantly being sidelined.

'Right or left arm, Mr Hope?' she asked tightly.

'Left, seeing as how I'm right-handed,' he replied, taking off his jacket and beginning to roll up his sleeve. 'You know, I never would have said Mairi Morrison kept a dirty house, but, then, nobody knows what goes on behind other folk's closed doors, do they, and—?'

'TB is not caused by dirt, Mr Hope,' Jess declared irritably as she struggled to her feet. 'It's caused by a fungus-like bacteria called Mycobacterium tuberculosis—'

'Homeless people and alcoholics get it, too, don't they?' he said. 'I suppose, living alone all these years, she probably started drinking a little in the evening, then it progressed to drinking during the day—'

'Mr Hope, Mairi Morrison is *not* an alcoholic!' Jess exclaimed, her green eyes flashing, 'and if I hear anyone suggesting she might be, I'm going to know exactly who started the rumour!'

He didn't look the least bit ashamed, but she wasn't surprised. Nothing short of a sledgehammer—and she had grave reservations about the efficacy of even that—was ever going to halt Wattie Hope in his relentless pursuit of gossip.

'I...um...this test—I thought it was given by injection, Doctor?' he said, nervously eyeing the metal spring-loaded instrument she had taken out of the cupboard.

He could have had an injection. They'd been injecting the tuberculin into the island children because it was less frightening for them, but Jess was damned if she was going to make this any easier for Wattie.

'Oh, come along now, Mr Hope,' she said bracingly. 'I'm sure a man of your age and experience won't mind a little discomfort.'

He shrank back in his seat, looking even more weasel-like than usual. 'And...ah...exactly how much discomfort are we talking about here?'

'Hardly any at all, really.' She smiled. A small, false smile which had Wattie swallowing convulsively. 'Well, not too much at any rate. Once I've placed a tiny drop of tuberculin—that's a purified protein extracted from the bacteria which causes tuberculosis—onto your forearm, I'm going to use this...' Deliberately she waved the spring-loaded device under his nose. 'It has a circle of *very* sharp prongs at the end of it to force the tuberculin into your skin through a mass of tiny puncture holes.'

He looked at her, then at the spring-loaded instrument, then quickly pulled down his sleeve and reached for his jacket. 'I think I might wait until you send me out a screening invitation, Doctor. Surgeries are supposed to be for consultations, aren't they? I really shouldn't be taking up your time like this.'

'No, you shouldn't, but as you're here—'

She didn't get a chance to finish. Wattie shot out the door with a speed that suggested his bad back had been miraculously cured.

A bubble of laughter sprang from her lips, laughter which quickly died when she placed his folder in her already full out-box. OK, so terrifying Wattie witless by wildly exaggerating how painful the test was might have given her temporary satisfaction, but if she'd simply administered it at least it would have been one less. One less amongst so many.

It was all taking so long, that was the trouble. She and Cath had been running screening clinics every afternoon for the past four days while Ezra did the home visits, and then in the evenings Cath and Ezra supervised a further clinic while she took the surgery, but they'd still only managed to see one hundred and sixty-five islanders. And even those one hundred and sixty-five tests were incomplete. The tuberculin took three to four days to take effect. Three to four days before they knew who had tested positive to it and who had tested negative.

'Jess, could you come through to Reception for a minute, please?'

Wearily Jess leant forward and pressed the answering button on her intercom. 'I'll be right along, Cath.'

'Fine.'

Cath didn't sound fine. In fact, Cath didn't look well either. Very white and drawn, as though she was sleeping badly. She was doing too much—they all were—but the last thing Jess wanted was Cath going off sick. Not now, and not when their new locum was due in a week. A new locum who would know neither the area nor any patients.

Ezra offered to stay on to help, her little voice pointed out as she made her way down the corridor towards the waiting room, but you told him you didn't want him. That you'd rather manage alone.

And she would, she told herself. OK, so three doctors would have completed the tests faster, but...

'I don't need him,' she muttered out loud. 'He's arrogant. He's insufferable and...'

Yet you're still attracted to him, her heart whispered when she reached the waiting room and saw him deep in conversation with Cath.

She was, and she despised herself for it. How *could* she still be attracted to a man who clearly considered general practice the bottom rung of the medical profession? How *could* her heart continue to skip a beat over a man who would far rather abandon medicine altogether than become a GP?

Because I'm an idiot, she thought as she hopped towards Cath, and knew it was true.

'Right, Cath, about this problem of yours—'

'You *promised*!' the receptionist exclaimed, her eyes flying immediately to Ezra. 'You said you wouldn't—'

'And I haven't,' he murmured. 'Not a word yet, believe me.'

Jess glanced from Cath to Ezra, then back again in confusion. 'Maybe I should go out and come back in again because I sure as heck don't know what you're talking about.'

'It's just a misunderstanding, that's all,' Ezra said smoothly. 'What can we do for you?'

'I was under the impression it was the other way round,' Jess said, still bewildered. '"Could you come through to Reception for a minute?" Cath said, and so I have.'

'Oh! Right, yes,' her receptionist replied, her cheeks darkening. 'It's...' Quickly she hunted through the phone messages on her desk. 'Hildy Wells. She wants to know if she can have a repeat prescription for her hormone replacement therapy.'

And maybe Hildy did, but Jess still wanted to know what she'd said to cause such consternation. 'Cath—'

'Inverlairg Health Centre,' the receptionist intoned as she answered the phone. 'Oh, good morning, Miss Brunton... Dr Arden?' Jess shook her head frantically at her, and Cath grinned. 'I'm sorry, but she's busy right now. Yes, by all means send her another catalogue, but I think we're pretty well stocked for pharmaceutical supplies at the moment.'

'That woman is making me feel like a prisoner in my own surgery,' Jess protested when Cath replaced the receiver. 'Doesn't she ever give up?'

'I read somewhere that pharmaceutical reps have to pass a series of aptitude tests before they're hired,' Ezra commented. 'Apparently, possessing a skin like a rhinoceros and the total inability to understand the word ''No'' are the two top priorities.'

'I can believe it,' Jess said with feeling. 'Cath—'

'What about Hildy's prescription? Can I tell her yes, or...?'

Jess frowned. 'Tell her I'd like to see her first. Her blood pressure was up the last time I checked it, and I want to monitor her.'

'Will I have to make an appointment, too, Dr Dunbar?' Fraser Kennedy asked as he joined them at the reception desk. 'I'm needing a repeat prescription for the cream you gave me. I'm going through tons of the stuff at the moment, trying to ease the pain.'

And he'd go through tons more, Jess thought, carefully avoiding Ezra's eyes as he told Fraser he didn't need to make an appointment. She couldn't perform Fraser's operation—standing for any length of time at the moment was completely impossible—and knowing what she now knew about Ezra, he couldn't do it either.

'Heavens, Jess, you look like you need a good night's sleep,' Fraser continued with a frown as Ezra went round the reception desk to get a prescription pad.

'I am a bit tired,' she admitted, but he shook his head.

'Stressed to hell, more like, and I'm not surprised. The way everyone's carrying on at the moment you'd think we had an outbreak of plague instead of one poor woman with TB.'

She nodded ruefully. 'The trouble is, people panic—'

'The trouble is, you take too much on yourself,' he declared, putting his arm round her shoulders and giving her a hug. 'Always did and, no doubt, always will.'

She smiled up at him. 'Probably. Fraser—'

'Your repeat prescription, Mr Kennedy,' Ezra said, thrusting it towards him.

'My offer still stands, you know,' Fraser continued, pocketing Ezra's prescription but keeping his eyes fixed firmly on Jess. 'Any time. Just say the word.'

As Jess looked deeply embarrassed, Ezra knew he didn't have to ask what offer Fraser Kennedy might have made, and he felt his heart twist with jealousy.

The big fisherman had it all, he thought, watching him leave. Good looks, his own business, a future. Jess would marry him for sure and live happily ever after, raising a whole family of little Kennedys, while he... He would return to the mainland, and try—somehow—to pretend he'd never ever met a girl called Jess Arden.

'So what's it to be, Ezra?'

'S-sorry?' he stammered, realising that both Cath and Jess were gazing at him expectantly.

'Robb MacGregor is down in the appointment book as my next patient,' Jess declared impatiently, 'but you said you'd like to see him when he came in for the results of his tests. Unless, of course, you're not interested any more?'

'Of course I'm still interested,' he protested, hearing the decided edge to her voice.

'Good. That's finally got that sorted out,' Cath said with relief. 'OK, Jess, you've got Grace Henderson next. Bad cold, and she thinks it might be turning into bronchitis.'

Without a word Jess took the folder Cath was holding

out to her, beckoned to Grace Henderson, then disappeared down the corridor, leaving Ezra staring after her.

She was still angry with him. He could see it, feel it. Angry because of what he'd said the night they'd met Trevor Taylor.

And she had every right to be angry. Hell, having done the work of a GP for almost a month, he had nothing but admiration for them, and for Jess in particular. The way she juggled the demands on her time—part doctor, part social worker, part psychiatrist—but it wasn't for him. His dream had always been to become a surgeon, and to do anything else…well, it was unthinkable.

'Dr Arden given me up as a lost cause, has she?' Robb MacGregor asked with a poor attempt at a smile after Ezra told him that the results from the infirmary had indicated he didn't have a peptic ulcer.

'No, of course not,' Ezra replied reassuringly. 'It's just that we're rather busy at the moment, but if you'd prefer to make another appointment to see Dr Arden, to discuss your case with her…?'

'Frankly, Doctor, I'd be prepared to see a chimpanzee if it could make me feel any better,' Robb sighed.

'No improvement, I take it?'

The builder shook his head. 'The diarrhoea's worse, my legs have started swelling up like balloons and I've got a rash now, too.'

Somewhere in the back of Ezra's mind a memory stirred of a lecture he'd attended years ago when he'd been a student. 'What sort of rash—where?'

'On my knees,' Robb MacGregor replied, rolling up his trouser legs to show him. 'It's like a whole load of tiny red blisters, and this morning the wife noticed there were some on my back, too.'

As Ezra stared down at the blisters on Robb MacGregor's knees he suddenly realised he might just have discovered what was wrong with the man.

* * *

'Coeliac disease?' Jess paused in the act of reaching for her cup of coffee. 'You think Robb might have coeliac disease, but—'

'Think about it, Jess,' Ezra said eagerly. 'His constant fatigue, the diarrhoea and stomach pain. And now his legs are swelling, and he's got blisters on his knees and back. I know gluten intolerance is something normally associated with children—'

'But it can develop in adults.' She nodded. 'Adults who have eaten wheat and rye all their lives and never had any ill effects before.'

'And it would also explain his weight loss,' Ezra continued. 'If the lining of his small intestine is being damaged by the gluten in his diet, it won't be absorbing any nutrients.'

'Yes, but—'

'And it would explain all his vague, apparently unrelated symptoms. In adults an intolerance to gluten can take months—even years—to manifest itself.'

She took a sip of her coffee, and stared at him thoughtfully. 'You're really excited about this, aren't you?'

'Because it *fits*, Jess,' he exclaimed. 'The poor man's had such a wretched time lately, and if I've cracked it—found out what's wrong—coeliac disease is so easy to treat. A simple change in diet...' He paused, seeing her smile. 'What—what's funny?'

'Just that being a GP isn't all about dishing out pills and treating people with piles and verrucas, is it?'

He coloured. 'Jess, what I said—'

'Forget it,' she said dismissively. 'The most important thing right now is to find out if you're right. Have you told Robb we'll have to make an appointment for him to have a jejunal biopsy?'

He nodded. 'I've explained it all to him. That he'll have to swallow a lubricated Crosby capsule attached to a length of tubing which will be guided down into his duodenum to suck up a small piece of tissue for analysis.'

'Did you also tell him he'll need to repeat this procedure three times?' she queried. 'Once after he's been eating a diet containing gluten, the next time when he's been on a gluten-free diet and the third time after gluten has been re-introduced into his diet?'

'He said he didn't care how often he had to do it just so long as we eventually found out what was wrong with him. I phoned the infirmary as soon as he left, stressed it was an urgent case, and the secretary said she'd try to get him an appointment for Tuesday.'

'*Tuesday?*' She shook her head. 'Ezra, I don't care what the hospital secretary told you, this is Saturday and Robb hasn't a hope in hell of getting an appointment for Tuesday. Three months on Tuesday, maybe, but not this Tuesday.'

His lips curved. 'Oh, I think he'll get an appointment. You see, I happened to mention where I used to work—what I did before…'

'And the poor woman became putty in your hands.' She laughed. 'Oh, *well done*, Ezra! I'm going to let you handle all our appointments in future. With you at the end of the phone our patients will be home and dry!'

Except, of course, that they wouldn't be, she suddenly realised. Because in the future he wouldn't be here.

The same thought must have occurred to him. All the enthusiasm and pleasure she'd seen in his face vanished in an instant, and it was a relief to both of them when Tracy popped her head round the consulting-room door.

'I've got your list of home visits ready, Ezra. You did say you wanted to get out on the road fast today, didn't you?' she added uncertainly, seeing him sigh.

He nodded, but when Tracy had closed the door he cleared his throat awkwardly. 'Jess…before I go, there's something I think you should know—'

'I'd forget my head if it wasn't screwed on!' Tracy laughed, appearing round the door again. 'I also meant to say that the first of this afternoon's screening session have arrived.'

'Already?' Jess protested, glancing up at her wall clock. 'But it's not even one o'clock!'

'Yeah, I know.' Tracy grimaced. 'No rest for the weary or the wicked, eh?'

There wasn't, and Jess reached for her crutches with a sigh, then remembered. 'Ezra, did you say there was something you wanted to talk to me about?'

He opened his mouth, closed it again and shook his head. 'It'll keep.'

She nodded. Judging by the sound of car doors slamming outside in the car park, she and Cath were in for yet another exhausting afternoon and, like he said, whatever he wanted to talk to her about would keep.

'I've never been so glad to see five o'clock,' Jess exclaimed, stretching her back to try to ease the stiffness. 'How many tests did we manage, Cath?'

The receptionist flicked through the cards on her desk. 'Thirty-eight. Sorry—thirty-nine. That makes two hundred and four we've done so far.'

'Only another three hundred and ninety-six to go,' Jess said ruefully. 'No, leave that,' she continued as Cath began filing the cards. 'I'll do it. You get off home.'

'Are you sure?' Cath said uncertainly. 'It would only take me a few minutes—'

'You've done enough,' Jess said firmly, taking the index cards from her. 'Go on—go home. Rebecca will be forgetting what you look like.'

Cath chuckled, slipped on her coat and began walking towards the surgery door, only to turn back a little uncertainly. 'Jess…'

'Mmm?' she murmured absently.

'I just… I only wanted you to know that I've really enjoyed working with you these last three years.'

But? There had been a definite *but* in there and Jess gazed at her in dismay. 'Oh, Cath, don't tell me you're going to resign! I know things have been tough recently, and I've been a real pig to you—'

'Of course I'm not going to resign—at least not willingly,' Cath protested. 'I just... I only wanted you to know that no matter what happens now, or...or in the future, I've had a great time, working with you.'

'I've enjoyed working with you, too,' Jess said, bewildered. 'In fact, I hope we'll have a lot more years together.'

'So do I.'

'Cath—'

'I'd better go,' her receptionist interrupted. 'Like you said, Rebecca will be forgetting what I look like.'

And before Jess could say anything else Cath had gone, leaving her bemused, confused and totally bewildered.

What the heck had all that been about?

Cath had sounded for all the world as though she'd been about to resign, then had told her she'd no intention of doing so, only to finish off by implying she might not be working for her for much longer.

Jess shook her head as she began filing the index cards. She was too tired to figure it out. She'd ask Cath about it tomorrow. No, not tomorrow. Tomorrow was Sunday. She'd ask her on Monday.

Or maybe she'd ask Ezra, she thought, hearing the sound of his car drawing to a halt outside the surgery. He'd been talking to Cath this morning, so maybe he knew what was going on.

'Ready to go?' he asked as he came into the office.

'Almost.' Silently she watched him as he put the patient folders he always took out with him on his home visits back into the filing cabinet. 'Rough afternoon?'

'Not particularly. I called in on Denise Fullarton on my way back.'

'And?'

'She's staying in her bed as we suggested, and she's still pregnant.'

So why did he look so depressed? As though something was bothering him. 'Ezra—'

'Do you still want to drop in at the Sinclair Memorial—see how Mairi is?'

'Yes. I won't stay long—just for a few minutes,' she added quickly, seeing him frown. 'Fiona says she's responding well to the treatment but she can't get her interested in anything, and I thought if I spoke to her...'

For a second she thought he was going to argue with her—he looked as though he'd like to—but instead he simply led the way out to his car and helped her in.

'How many tests did you manage to get through this afternoon?' he asked as he drove through Inverlairg's narrow streets towards the hospital.

'Thirty-nine. Cath and I were hoping to make it fifty, but we had some no-shows.'

'Hopefully that means the panic's beginning to die down,' he said. 'People not turning up, I mean.'

They could only hope so, Jess thought as they arrived at the Sinclair Memorial. For Mairi's sake, as well as their own.

'Have you both been vaccinated against TB?' she asked as soon as she saw them. 'Because if you haven't—'

'Mairi, relax,' Jess interrupted gently. 'You can't give us TB. We just came to see how you are.'

'Fine. I'm fine.'

She didn't look fine. She looked tired, and depressed, and haunted. Quickly Jess sat down on the edge of her bed, and to her dismay Mairi deliberately moved further away from her.

'How are you getting on with the pills we're giving you?' Jess asked, determinedly bright. 'Any rash—itchiness?'

'I'm fine, I told you,' Mairi replied irritably, then shook her head at Ezra. 'You should have taken this girl straight home. She looks about dead on her feet.'

He smiled. 'Have you ever tried telling this girl *anything*, Mairi?'

To Jess's relief Mairi chuckled.

'Aye, she's an argumentative one, and no mistake. Never did know when to give in gracefully, and still doesn't.'

'I'm *not* argumentative,' Jess protested. 'I…I simply have strong opinions—'

'*Strong?*' Ezra gasped. 'Mairi, this girl's opinions were formed at the same time as the Ten Commandments. This girl would argue black was white rather than admit she was wrong.'

'And this man is so arrogant he thinks GPs treat nothing but piles and verrucas,' Jess declared, happily entering into the spirit of things if only to keep Mairi smiling. 'I blame his parents. They should have sat on him years ago, and then I wouldn't have to endure his half-baked ideas!'

To Jess's surprise the amusement disappeared instantly from Mairi's face, to be replaced by consternation. 'You haven't told her, then, lad?'

'Told me what?' Jess said, glancing from Mairi to Ezra in confusion.

'It doesn't matter,' he said dismissively. 'It's old history now anyway.'

'Your past's never just history, lad,' Mairi said softly. 'It's what made you the person you are.'

He didn't look convinced, and Jess cleared her throat. 'Ezra, if I've said something I shouldn't—'

'Of course you haven't,' he interrupted. 'My parents were killed in a car crash when I was four, that's all, and I was brought up in an orphanage.'

Jess wished the ground would open up and swallow her. 'Ezra, I'm sorry…'

'It doesn't matter,' he insisted. 'Despite what Mairi said, it's no big deal.'

Oh, but it was, she thought. And it explained so much. His air of complete self-reliance, the way he'd defined himself solely in relationship to his skill. It told her a lot more about him that he could ever have realised.

'Do you remember your parents at all?' she asked gently.

His mother's hands. He remembered them. Soft, slender, wiping away his tears after he'd fallen over and hurt himself. And his father's arms. Big, strong, picking him up, holding him.

'No, I don't remember them,' he replied.

She didn't believe him. He could see she didn't, just as he could also see sympathy in her large green eyes, and he didn't want that. For the past thirty years he'd survived by needing no one, depending on no one, and he didn't want to need someone now. Wanting Jess was a simple, biological fact of life—but needing her… No, he couldn't cope with that.

He got to his feet, anxious to escape those soft green eyes. 'I've left my car out front. Hopefully we won't get any emergencies, but if we do, I'm blocking the access.'

And before either woman could say anything he was gone.

'You like him—a lot, I mean, don't you?' Mairi observed.

Jess smiled a little ruefully. 'Yes—yes, I do.'

'Maybe you could persuade him to stay on—join you in the practice?'

Jess shook her head. 'The practice doesn't make enough money to support two doctors, you know that, Mairi.'

And it didn't, but neither did Jess add what she also knew to be true. That there was nothing on Greensay for Ezra—nothing that could possibly tempt him to stay.

But Mairi wasn't about to let it go. 'He's got black hair, Jess. Perhaps—under that dreadful beard—he's also got the cleft chin?'

Jess laughed shakily. 'Even if he has… Even if I wanted… We're just colleagues, that's all.'

'Well, all I can say is you're a fool,' Mairi declared firmly. 'Because if I had Ezra Dunbar staying with me, and

I was twenty years younger, I wouldn't be letting him walk out of my life, that's for sure!'

Which was easy for Mairi to say, Jess thought when Ezra returned and Mairi urged them both to get off home. But how could you interest a man who wasn't interested in you? You couldn't.

Especially when that man seemed even more indifferent than usual, she decided sadly as she shared her evening meal with him some time later. Normally, he would at least try to make some conversation, perhaps about a patient's medical background or a condition he felt he didn't know enough about, but tonight—nothing. Nothing but the occasional request to pass the salt, or an 'Excuse me' when he went to collect their next course from the kitchen.

It was a relief when their meal was over, and deliberately she picked up her crutches. 'I think—if you don't mind— I might just go to bed.'

'Could you wait just a minute?' he asked. 'There's something I want to say to you. Something I've been putting off since this morning, and I really do want to get it over with.'

'That sounds ominous.' She smiled but he, she noticed, didn't.

'It's about Cath. She came to see me this morning—'

'She wants to resign, doesn't she?' Jess interrupted. 'We had a really garbled conversation this afternoon, and I thought then that she was trying to pluck up the courage—'

'Jess, she came to see me as a patient. She…' He bit his lip. 'She has a lump—in her breast.'

'A lump?'

'Jess, it's probably nothing more sinister than a cyst caused by a blocked duct in her breast,' he continued swiftly, seeing the shock in her face. 'Or a fibroadenoma— a collection of fibrous glandular tissue which has become knotted together to form a solid lump. She's only forty, and breast cancer usually affects women over the age of fifty.'

'But it can affect younger women,' she murmured. 'Her mother died from breast cancer—one of her aunts, too.'

'And you're already jumping two steps ahead,' he protested. 'All we know right now is that she's got a lump in her breast. I've made an appointment for her to have a mammogram and a needle aspiration on Monday. It'll be time enough to start worrying then if they find something to worry about.'

'You said she was looking tired,' Jess continued as though Ezra hadn't spoken, 'and I dismissed it—said it was just because Rebecca was playing up. Oh, hell, Ezra, I was so horrible to her when she lost Mairi's test results, and all the time she must have known about the lump, been worrying about it…'

'Jess, you've got a lot on your plate at the moment,' he said, hating the distress he could see in her eyes. 'Everyone gets bad-tempered at times—'

'She came to you. She had a lump in her breast, and yet she came to you. Cath and I are friends. We go back years.'

'Maybe that's why she wanted to see someone else. Sometimes it's easier to talk to a stranger.'

'And Mairi—what about Mairi?' she continued. 'I've known her since I was a child, and yet it was you who persuaded her to have treatment, not me. And Robb MacGregor. It wasn't me who found out what was wrong with him.'

'Jess, I only *think* he might have coeliac's disease,' he declared. 'And if you'd seen his rash this morning I'm sure that thought would have occurred to you, too.'

'Would it, Ezra—*would* it?' she said unhappily. 'I chewed off your head when you said I shouldn't try to fill my father's shoes—that I couldn't do it—but you were right. I'm a failure, aren't I? A failure as a GP.'

'Hey, stop that right now,' he demanded, grasping her firmly by the shoulders. 'You're a bloody marvellous GP!'

'Cath obviously didn't think so.'

'Cath thinks you're wonderful. She just didn't want to land you with any more stress.'

Tears welled in her eyes. 'Didn't she?'

He grasped her chin in his hand and forced her to look up at him. 'Jess, if Cath were in your situation—with a fractured leg, a measles epidemic and a possible TB outbreak pending—would you want to add to her problems?'

'No, but—'

'Jess, would I lie to you?'

His voice was soft, and unbelievably tender, and the tears she'd been trying to hold in check began spilling down her cheeks.

Gently—oh, so gently—he wiped them away with his fingers, his eyes deep with understanding. For a second— a brief, fleeting second—she thought he might take her into his arms and hold her—and she desperately needed to be held—but he didn't.

Instead he reached for her crutches and said gruffly, 'I think you should go to bed now. It's been a long day, and you need sleep.'

She stared up at him for a moment, then slowly turned away. Yes, she needed sleep, but with an aching heart she also realised something else. This man had never held her unless she'd asked him to, had never once kissed her—not even as a friend—and yet she was in love with him, and it was a love that was going nowhere.

CHAPTER EIGHT

'CATH, just because the infirmary has expressed concern about the cells they removed from your breast yesterday, it doesn't automatically mean you have cancer.'

'I know,' her receptionist replied, staring down at her hands as she sat in Jess's consulting room.

'The surgical biopsy they want to perform on Saturday is a pretty standard procedure. They'll remove the lump under a general anaesthetic—'

'Jess, I was a theatre sister at the Sinclair Memorial for ten years, I know what's going to happen. Which is why…' Cath's head came up and she met Jess's gaze full on '…I'm only going to give them permission to do the biopsy—nothing more.'

Jess glanced across at Ezra in dismay and he leant forward in his seat quickly. 'Do you think that's wise, Cath?'

'You think I should just let them remove part—or all—of my breast on Saturday if the lump turns out to be cancerous?'

'If they consider it necessary—'

'It's my body, Ezra, and nothing's going to happen to it until I've looked at every option and decided what's best for me.'

He would talk her round, Jess thought confidently, watching him. He would explain that sometimes surgery was the *only* option, but to her dismay he merely gazed at Cath thoughtfully for a second, then nodded. 'It's your decision.'

'Ezra—'

'You heard what Cath said. It's her body.'

'Yes, but—'

'Have you told your husband and daughter why you're going into hospital this weekend?' he continued, turning his attention back to Cath.

'Peter knows—he's flying back tomorrow from the Gulf—but Rebecca...' Cath shook her head. 'I don't know whether to tell her or not. She's only fourteen...'

'Tell her,' Ezra declared emphatically. 'If this scare turns out to be a false alarm she can share in your joy and relief. If it doesn't... Believe me, it will be a hell of a lot harder if you have to tell her later.'

Cath glanced across at Jess, and she nodded. 'I agree. Rebecca's old enough to understand, and if you keep something like this from her she'll feel hurt and excluded if you do have to tell her eventually.'

'I suppose so,' Cath murmured, then got to her feet. 'I'd better get back to work. The waiting room's packed again this morning.'

'Which is why I really do wish you'd take the rest of the week off,' Jess said.

'And do what?' Cath said. 'Sit around staring at my breasts for the next three days, wondering if I'm still going to have two in a month's time? I'd far rather keep busy.'

And before either of them could reply, she was gone.

'She'll be all right, Jess, no matter what happens,' Ezra said, his eyes fixed on her sympathetically. 'She's got a good attitude, and if her lump *does* turn out to be cancerous there are so many ways we can fight this disease nowadays.'

'I know—I *do* know that, but...' Jess threw down her pen with frustration. 'Why didn't you talk her into letting the infirmary do whatever they think best on Saturday? If she does have breast cancer she'll have to go through the trauma of two operations—'

'Only if she decides that surgery is what she wants. Jess, you heard what she said,' he said as she began to protest. 'And as a nurse she probably knows as much about the disease as we do. If the biopsy result isn't good, we can give her our support and opinion, but that's all we can do. The final decision has to be hers.'

A little under five weeks ago it would never have occurred to him that Cath might have rights, opinions, and Jess wished with all her heart that he was still in that state of happy ignorance. That he'd simply steamrollered the receptionist into undergoing whatever surgery was necessary.

'We're not gods, remember?' he said, clearly reading her mind. 'I've had to learn that the hard way. My arrogance cost me my career. Yours is going to cost you your health if you're not careful.'

'I'm not arrogant,' she exclaimed. 'I'm just worried about Cath.'

'I know you are, but I'm not talking about Cath—or at least not solely. It's this practice. It's a form of arrogance to think you can run it on your own, and I'd have thought these past few weeks would have shown you that you can't.'

'I don't make a habit of breaking my leg,' she protested.

'No, but you're on call twenty-four hours a day, seven days a week, and nobody can keep up that level of commitment. Not if they want to remain sane.'

'My father—'

'Didn't face anything like the pressures you've got,' he interrupted. 'Ten—even five years ago—there were conditions we simply couldn't treat, but now there's a treatment for just about anything, and if you try to provide it alone—without help—it will kill you.'

He was right. Deep down she knew he was, but...

'Even if what you're saying is true,' she murmured, 'there aren't enough people on Greensay to pay for another full-time doctor.'

'Then advertise for someone to work part time with you. Advertise, interview and appoint someone to help you.'

It made sense—she knew it did—but she didn't want to advertise. She didn't want to interview. There was only one doctor she wanted to help her—one man she wanted in her life—and he didn't want to be there.

Her intercom crackled into life.

'Jess, I'm sorry to disturb you,' Tracy said, sounding distinctly harassed, 'but the natives are getting pretty restless out here. We're already running twenty minutes late and—'

Ezra leant forward and pressed the intercom button. 'We're just coming, Tracy.'

'Your discussion with Cath's over, then?'

Ezra smiled across at Jess. The girl was clearly eaten up with curiosity, but it was for Cath to decide how much she should know. 'Yes, our discussion's over,' he said, flicking off the intercom. Quickly he got to his feet, then paused. 'Why don't you ask your locum if she'd like to stay on permanently?'

'She's a he, and I don't think a young man of twenty-six is going to be interested in part-time work.'

Ezra's dark eyebrows snapped together. 'I thought the agency was sending you a woman?'

She shrugged. 'They must be all out of them at the moment. He sounded very nice on the phone,' she added, seeing his frown deepen.

'You've spoken to him?'

'Considering he's arriving on Saturday night, it would have been a bit odd if I *hadn't*, don't you think?' she declared. 'He phoned the surgery this morning and, like I said, he sounded very nice.'

'And where is this *very nice* locum going to live while he's here?' he asked with a decided edge.

'With me until I'm mobile again.'

'With you?' he said.

'He's hardly going to be much use if he stays on the other side of the island, is he?' Jess replied, more tartly than she'd intended. 'The whole point of him being here is to help me with home visits and night calls.'

'Yes, but...' He bit his lip. 'Jess, he's a stranger. He could...well, he could take advantage. He could—'

'Sweet talk me with flattering words, and seduce me into his bed?' she suggested, beginning to get seriously annoyed. 'For God's sake, Ezra, you've been living with me for almost five weeks and it hasn't turned you into a rampant sexual predator with lustful designs on my body!'

Just how wrong could she be? he thought. Hell's teeth, didn't she realise how close to the edge he'd come on several occasions? Obviously not. And as for her crackpot assumption that as *he* hadn't taken advantage, no other man would...

'Jess, listen to me—'

'Not when you're talking such utter nonsense I won't!' she retorted, grabbing hold of her crutches and hitching them up under her arms. 'Good grief, try for a bit of common sense. What young man of twenty-six is going to harbour lustful, lascivious thoughts towards a plain, ordinary woman of thirty-two with a broken leg?'

Plain? *Ordinary?* Didn't she know her red curls framed a face that was achingly attractive? Didn't she realise that her green eyes glowed when she laughed, or that she had the cutest way of wrinkling her nose when she was puzzled?

'Jess—'

'Ezra, he comes with the very best of references, not to mention two glowing letters of recommendation from GPs he's worked with before,' she said, hopping angrily out of her room so he had no choice but to follow her. 'I'm the one who's going to work with him, and if I thought he sounded nice on the phone, that should be an end to the matter!'

But it wasn't, Ezra thought grimly. 'Nice' suggested this man had already insinuated his way into her good graces. 'Nice' suggested that once he was actually living with her it would only be a matter of time before...

'Jess...'

Pointedly she pushed open the waiting-room door. 'We have patients waiting, Ezra.'

He opened his mouth, then closed it again. That he was itching to continue the conversation was obvious. That he intended arguing with her was plain. But she'd had enough. The nerve of the man. The sheer, unadulterated nerve! Suggesting her new locum might have the morals of an alley cat. Implying she would be easy game for him if he did. If Ezra considered her so easy, why the hell hadn't he taken advantage of her himself?

The sooner he was off the island, the better. The sooner her new locum arrived, the happier she'd be.

Only she wouldn't.

It's for the best, Jess, her heart whispered as he strode ahead of her to the reception desk, his face grim. He doesn't belong here, never would. You might think he'd make an excellent GP, but it isn't what he wants.

Neither are you.

'Mrs Henderson hasn't arrived yet, Jess,' Cath said as soon as she saw her. 'Do you want to give her another five minutes or…?'

'Who's next?'

'John Wilson.'

Jess frowned. John was suffering from deep depression, and his consultation couldn't be rushed. 'I'll give Grace another five minutes.'

Cath nodded. 'Sheila Murray, for you, Ezra. She's off on holiday to Africa in a couple of weeks and needs the usual vaccinations.'

'And I'm sure she's quite capable of telling me that herself, don't you?' he snapped.

Cath gazed at him, open-mouthed, but when he'd ushered Sheila and her small daughter away she turned to Jess, her eyebrows raised. 'Was it something I said?'

'You and me both,' Jess said with feeling, then shook her head as the receptionist's eyebrows climbed even higher. 'Forget it, Cath. He's just in a foul mood this morning.'

'Maybe it's because he's leaving at the end of the week,' Cath said thoughtfully. 'Maybe he'd like to stay on?'

Yeah, right, and pigs might fly, Jess thought glumly. He'd never so much as hinted he might like to stay on. Hadn't even expressed any interest in doing so.

She turned with a sigh as the surgery door clattered open and Grace Henderson hurried in, bringing with her an icy blast of air which had everyone in the waiting room quickly pulling their coats closer.

'I'm so sorry to be late, Doctor, but my son couldn't get the car started,' she gasped apologetically. 'And then some sheep were out on the road just beyond Colaboll farm so, of course, David had to get them all back in their field, and—'

'Relax, Grace,' Jess smiled. 'I'm not in any hurry.'

'Oh, *good*.' She beamed. 'Then you won't mind if I just nip into the ladies' toilet? It's the cold weather, you see,' she added, already halfway there. 'It plays havoc with my waterworks.'

'Why do I have the feeling it's going to be one of those days?' Cath groaned when the two phones on her desk began to ring simultaneously.

'If one of them is Virginia Brunton from Dawson's Pharmaceuticals, tell her I've emigrated,' Jess declared. 'Better yet, tell her…' The rest of what she'd been about to say died in her throat as Ezra suddenly came back into the waiting room, white-lipped with anger, while Sheila Murray hurried after him, frantically apologising, as her three-year-old daughter Amy howled at the top of her lungs. 'What on earth…?'

'Oh, damn,' Cath groaned, cradling one of the phones against her chest. 'I should have put Sheila on your list when I saw she had Amy with her, but I completely forgot.'

'Forgot what?' Jess said, puzzled.

'Bert Mackenzie, of course. Inverlairg Health Centre,'

she announced down the phone. 'Oh, hello, Mr Guthrie. You'd like to see Dr Dunbar tomorrow?' Her hand hovered over the appointment book. 'He won't be free until eleven forty-five, I'm afraid. Right… Fine. We'll see you then.'

'What about Bert Mackenzie?' Jess demanded, still confused.

Cath reached for the other phone. 'Don't tell me you've forgotten what happened at the Christmas party when Sheila put Amy on Santa Claus's knee?'

'You mean when she kicked the poor man black and blue because she was terrified of his beard, and Bert said he'd never volunteer to be Santa again?'

'Exactly.'

Jess gazed at Cath silently for a second, then her lip quivered. 'You think that because Ezra's got a beard, Amy…?'

Cath's own lip started to tremble. 'It looks awfully like it. Do you think I should explain—?'

'Not if you value your life, I don't.' Jess chuckled. 'Mind you, I can't say I entirely blame the child. I don't much like his beard either.'

'That child's bottom needs to be thoroughly tanned!' Ezra exclaimed furiously as he joined them. 'I took her on my knee—just to give her mother time to recover from her yellow fever jab—and she went crazy!'

'Amy can be a…a little unpredictable at times,' Jess replied with difficulty.

'*Unpredictable?* The words "walking menace" would be more accurate. It's *not* funny, Jess!' he continued, seeing her lips twitch.

'No, of course it's not,' she agreed. 'It's just…' Her rebellious lips refused to be stilled. 'Greensay now appears to have a matching set of limping doctors.'

He didn't look one bit amused. Instead, he grabbed the nearest file, glanced down at the name on it and barked, 'Aziz Singh!'

Indira jumped like a startled rabbit. So did the rest of the waiting room, and everyone kept their eyes fixed firmly on their magazines as she picked up her small son and followed Ezra to his consulting room.

'Boy, but he *is* in a foul mood,' Cath muttered. 'Got out of bed on the wrong side this morning, did he?'

'I wouldn't know,' Jess replied, then coloured as she suddenly realised how wistful she'd sounded. 'Look, would you mind bringing Grace along when she finally gets out of the toilet? My leg's really bothering me this morning.'

'Sure thing.' Cath nodded, but Jess knew her receptionist wasn't one bit deceived.

Why, oh, why couldn't she have fallen in love with Fraser Kennedy? she wondered with a deep sigh as she went into her consulting room and closed the door. Fraser would have married her tomorrow if she had but said the word, and yet she'd had to go and fall in love with a man who was bossy, overbearing and opinionated.

A man who would be leaving the island in four days.

How was she going to bear it?

Because you have to, her heart sighed. There's nothing else you can do.

A knock on her consulting-room door had her pasting a smile to her lips, but it wasn't Grace Henderson, as she'd expected. It was Cath, with Simon and Elspeth Ralston and their little boy, Toby, and they all looked worried.

'I'm sorry, Jess, but we seem to have a bit of an emergency here,' Cath said. 'Toby—'

'I think he's going blind, Doctor!' Elspeth exclaimed tearfully, clutching her son to her chest. 'His left eye looks all funny, and if he's going blind, I don't think I'll be able to bear it. He's so little—'

'Why don't you and your husband come in and sit down?' Jess interrupted, nodding to Cath who made a discreet exit to warn Grace she could be in for a lengthy wait. 'Now, Elspeth, take a deep breath and start at the beginning. When did you first think something was wrong with Toby's eyesight?'

'Yesterday—just after lunch,' she replied. 'I thought his eye looked a little bit red then, but Simon said he'd just poked his finger in it.'

'He's always doing that,' her husband said defensively. 'Or sticking things in his ear, or up his nose—'

'And how would you know?' Elspeth flared. 'The only reason you're home at the moment is because you hurt your hand on that damn boat. You're never here when I need you. Sailing all the hours God sends—'

'Is Toby's eye redder this morning than it was yesterday?' Jess asked, seeing the signs of a full-scale marital disagreement beginning.

Elspeth nodded. 'He wouldn't let me open the curtains when he got up—said the light hurt his eyes—and when he started walking into things, as though he couldn't see them properly—'

'His eye *looks* odd, too, Doctor,' Simon chipped in. 'The coloured bit doesn't seem as round as it should be, and it's a funny colour—not blue, like his other eye.'

'Does your eye hurt at all, Toby?' Jess asked gently. The little boy nodded, his bottom lip trembling, and she reached for her ophthalmoscope. 'Elspeth, could you keep him as still as you can for me? OK, Toby, I'm just going to shine this little torch in your eye for a second. It won't hurt, I promise,' she continued as he squirmed in his mother's arms, clearly not liking the idea one bit.

The white of Toby's eye was certainly very red, especially the area near the iris, and, as Simon had said, the iris itself wasn't quite as round or as blue as it should have been.

'You said you first noticed the redness yesterday?' Jess murmured.

Elspeth nodded.

'And how long has the eye been watering?'

'It started this morning.' Elspeth clutched her son tighter. 'Is…is he going blind, Doctor?'

Jess shook her head. 'He has iritis—an inflammation of

the coloured part of the eye. Attacks like this aren't uncommon in children with juvenile arthritis, but it usually clears up in a couple of weeks.'

'Then…it's not serious?' Elspeth asked, uncertainty and hope plain in her voice.

'It could have been if you'd ignored it, but all he needs is some corticosteroid cream.'

Elspeth gasped with relief. 'Oh, thank God! I thought… I was sure…'

'He'll be fine, Elspeth,' Jess insisted. 'I'll give you a prescription for the cream, but don't be over-generous with it. The tiniest amount is all that's needed.' Quickly she wrote out the prescription but when Simon took it from her she couldn't help but glance down at his fingers. 'Your hand's looking good, Simon. Do you mind if I take a look?'

Obediently he held out his hand to her. 'Dr Dunbar took out the stitches last week, and it seems OK, but I thought I'd have a lot more movement in it.'

Jess smiled reassuringly as she led the way out into the corridor. 'Once you start physiotherapy it will soon regain all its old mobility.'

Simon looked relieved, then coloured slightly as his wife shot him a speaking look. 'I never did thank you for speaking to Fraser Kennedy on my behalf, Doctor. I know I wouldn't have a job if it weren't for you.'

'Nonsense,' Jess protested. 'Fraser just recognises a good worker when he's got one.'

'Yeah, right, and I'm the tooth fairy.' Simon grinned. 'Without you and Dr Dunbar—well, I don't know what would have happened to me. Dr Dunbar's leaving at the end of the week, isn't he?'

Out of the corner of her eye Jess could see that Ezra had come out of his consulting room with Indira and Aziz.

'Dr Dunbar was only filling in temporarily, Simon, and Dr Walton has excellent references.'

'He's going to have to be pretty spectacular to be anything like as good as Dr Dunbar.'

He would, but Jess had no intention of going down that road, and certainly not with a patient. 'I'm sure everyone will soon get to know and like him,' she said firmly. 'I thought he sounded very nice on the phone.'

'Yes, but what does Dr Dunbar think?' Simon pressed. 'I mean, does he feel he's the right man for the job?'

Like Ezra's opinion should matter? she thought, fuming inwardly. Like a man who'd been a member of her practice for a little over four weeks was entitled to an opinion?

'Dr Dunbar thought he sounded perfect,' she declared tightly, all too aware that Ezra was listening and daring him to contradict her. 'In fact...in fact, he thinks Dr Walton will be a great asset to the practice.'

Like hell I do, Ezra thought grimly when Jess had disappeared into her consulting room. 'Asset' wasn't the word which sprang into his mind whenever he thought about Jess's new locum. It was something altogether more colourful and unprintable.

'I am so sorry to have bothered you unnecessarily, Doctor,' Indira murmured, her expression uncomfortable, embarrassed as he accompanied her back to the waiting room. 'Nazir said I must not—that you had enough to do with all the tuberculosis tests—'

'It's never a bother when a child of Aziz's age is unwell,' he replied quickly, smiling down at her and the little boy in her arms. 'OK, so this time he just has a bad case of toddler's diarrhoea, but it could have been something more serious, and you were wise to bring him in.'

Indira looked relieved. 'My neighbour said you would not think I was a nuisance.'

'Of course you're not,' Ezra protested.

'She is a nice girl, my neighbour,' Indira continued, 'but, then, I have met so many nice people ever since Nazir and I came to the island. Everyone has been so kind, so welcoming.'

Ezra nodded. 'Greensay's a pretty special place.'

'You have found that, too?' Indira said, her large, dark

eyes lighting up. 'I am so pleased for you, Doctor. I hoped you might be happy here, and it is good to hear you are.'

Happy? How in the world could Indira Singh possibly think he was *happy*? he wondered, staring after her as she left the surgery. Good grief, every day had been a nightmare since he'd joined Jess's practice. Facing conditions and ailments he hadn't come across since his pre-registrar year, frantically trying to dredge his memory for the right treatments. And then, on top of that, to find himself in the middle of a full-blown TB scare...!

But you're enjoying it, aren't you? a voice in his mind whispered. In a peculiar, masochistic way, you're actually enjoying it.

Yes, but enjoying a challenge wasn't the same as being happy, he argued as the day sped by in a chaotic round of consultations, home visits and then yet another evening tuberculin testing clinic.

In fact, the more he thought about it, the more he found himself wondering if there'd ever been a time in his life when he'd been truly happy.

Not as a child. As a child, his life had been dominated by pain, and grief, and an unutterable loneliness. Medicine—surgery—had been his lifeline when he'd grown up but, looking back on his career, he could see that though it had given him immense satisfaction, it had never brought him happiness. And yet here, on this tiny island in the back of beyond, doing work he would have mocked a year ago...

Then why don't you stay on here permanently—join Jess in the practice?

The thought popped into his head just as he completed his last tuberculin test, and he began to laugh inwardly at the absurdity of such an idea only to stop. Was it really such a crazy idea? It would be a new beginning, a way of starting over again. And if he stayed, he and Jess might marry...

Whoa, there, his brain protested. *Marry?* Right now, Jess

doesn't even *like* you. No, but if he stayed on here, maybe…maybe one day she might grow to love him as he loved her.

And he did love her, he suddenly realised. It wasn't just lust he felt for her now. It was something richer, deeper. An overwhelming longing to be with her always, to take care of her, to grow old with her.

And you can come right down out of cloud-cuckoo-land now and face reality, Ezra, his mental voice jeered. Even if Jess were to fall in love with you, what are you going to live on in this brand new Eden? The only work available is a part-time post at the health centre, and that wouldn't support you, far less a wife.

You could apply for the surgeon's job at the Sinclair Memorial, his heart whispered. Work there part time and the rest of the time with Jess.

He glanced down at his hands, and swore under his breath. Just the thought of walking into an operating theatre again was enough to make them tremble. No, he couldn't do that, and to live off Jess… No, he couldn't do that either.

'Gosh, do you realise it's after nine o'clock already?' Cath said as she joined him in his consulting room. 'How many did you manage to get done tonight?'

'Twenty-five.'

'And I've done twenty-two so that makes…' She wrinkled her nose in concentration. 'Three hundred and fifty-two. We've done three hundred and fifty-two all together. Mind you, right now, it feels more like three thousand!' She shook her head and chuckled, then glanced at him curiously. 'Are you OK, Ezra?'

No, he wasn't OK, but he could pretend it was. He'd got very good at pretending lately. Pretending he didn't want to make love to Jess, pretending he didn't feel anything when she smiled at him, when she was close to him.

Yes, he could go on pretending even though a part of him felt as though it were withering and dying, never to live again.

'Is Jess ready to go?' he asked abruptly.

'Yes, I'm ready,' she replied, appearing in his doorway, and as he strode past her the two women exchanged glances.

Both had been hoping he might be in a better frame of mind by the time he'd finished conducting the tuberculin tests, but he clearly wasn't.

'Want to come home to my house for dinner?' Cath muttered.

Jess was sorely tempted, but she shook her head. Cath had enough on her plate without cooking for an unexpected guest.

Which didn't mean she intended enduring Ezra's foul mood all evening, she decided when he helped her into the car then drove silently away from the surgery.

'Look, is it still the morals of my poor locum that's bugging you?' she demanded, 'or are you still in a huff with me because of Amy?'

It was neither, but he had no intention of telling her what was really on his mind so he said the first thing that came into his head. 'Do you really hate my beard?'

'Do I what?' she gasped, totally thrown.

'My beard. I heard you talking to Cath this morning.'

'I— No—of course I don't,' she floundered. 'It's just I've always had this theory…' Oh, hell, but she'd suddenly remembered what her theory was. 'Forget it. It's stupid, ridiculous.'

'What theory?'

He wouldn't let it drop—she knew he wouldn't—and she bit her lip. 'I've…I've always thought that men with beards were either chinless wonders or had something to hide. Look, I told you it was stupid,' she continued when he didn't reply. 'I said it was ridic— Why are we stopping?'

'Nazir doesn't close until half past nine on a Tuesday night and I want to buy a razor and some shaving cream.'

'But—'

'Jess, I grew this beard because I couldn't be bothered

to shave after I left the Royal,' he continued as she stared at him, open-mouthed, 'and I'm damned if I'm going to let you think I'm either hiding from my past or have a weak chin.'

'But—' He was gone before she could protest, and back again within minutes. 'Ezra, you don't have to do this—least of all to prove anything to me.'

'Oh, but I do. As soon as we get home, this…' he ran his fingers over his beard '…is going to come off, and then we'll see who has to eat her words!'

He's gone nuts, she thought as he drove her home then disappeared into the bathroom as soon as he'd put their dinner into the microwave. What difference did it make whether he had a beard or not? OK, so she didn't particularly like it, but to shave it off now?

Nuts. Living on Greensay had driven him nuts, and living with her had pushed him over the edge.

A bubble of laughter sprang to her lips. Maybe she should warn the new locum. Maybe she should ring him up—

'OK, what do you think?'

Jess turned, laughter still welling in her throat, and her jaw dropped.

'Hey, I don't look that bad without the beard, do I?' he said uncertainly, a dull flush of colour creeping across his freshly shaven cheeks as she continued to stare at him, stunned.

'No—no, of course you don't. It's just—'

'Look, I can always grow it back—'

'Oh, don't do that,' she said quickly. 'It's just… You…you've got a cleft chin.'

'So?' Ezra was clearly puzzled, and she felt herself blushing.

'It's…nice.'

'Nice?'

She nodded. 'When I was younger, I used to think—I

mean, I've always liked...' Lord, she wasn't making any sense. 'It's...nice.'

A smile curved his lips. 'I didn't realise Greensay's doctor had a thing about cleft chins.'

She managed a wobbly chuckle. 'There's a lot of things you don't know about me.'

'So it seems.'

His voice was deep, husky, and her eyes flew up to his. All amusement had gone from his face. Instead, there was something else there. Something which caused her breath to lodge tight in her throat and her heart begin to race very fast.

She swallowed, and saw his eyes widen and darken, then slowly, as though in a dream, his hands came up to cup her face. She didn't move—scarcely dared breathe. All she was aware of was the insistent hammering of her heart against her ribcage, the feeling that time itself was holding its breath and the insistent little voice in her head that was pleading, Kiss me. Please, please, kiss me.

And as though he heard that little voice, his lips were suddenly on hers, demanding, entreating, and she was kissing him back with equal desperation, wrapping her arms around him to bring him closer, closer.

'Jess... Oh, God, Jess!' he gasped, his voice choked, ragged as he showered her face with kisses.

His lips found hers again, and she moaned and arched against him, scarcely noticing when her blouse disappeared, then the fine wisp of her bra. But when his lips left hers and travelled down to her breasts, teasing them, tasting them, drawing each nipple into his mouth with an aching slowness, she cried out in ecstasy.

'Yes...Oh, yes!'

He kissed her again, drawing her close to him so she could feel the patent evidence of his hard arousal. 'I want.... Oh, Jess, you must know what I want, but—'

'Don't stop,' she begged, capturing his mouth with her own. 'Don't...Oh, please...don't stop!' His tongue delved deep, sending waves of pulsing sensation coursing through her, and she strained against him, knowing she wanted more, much more, only to groan with frustration when she heard her telephone begin to ring. 'Leave it—don't answer it!'

'I have to—you know I do,' he replied, his voice hoarse, his breathing rapid.

And he did, but as soon as Jess heard it was Fred Graham, her heart sank. His catheter had come loose again—it was always coming loose—and Fred panicked if he got so much as a splinter in his finger so it was going to be a long night.

'Don't wait up for me,' Ezra said, clearly reading her mind as he reached for his bag.

'Of course I will.'

'No, don't.'

'But—'

'Jess…' She looked confused, and he couldn't blame her. 'Jess, that phone call—stopping us. Perhaps it was for the best.'

'The best?' she repeated blankly.

'I'm leaving on Saturday afternoon. Not just the practice, this house. I'm leaving the island. I've bought a ticket for the four o'clock ferry.'

'But you don't have to go,' she said, horribly aware that she sounded as though she was begging but quite unable to stop herself. 'You've leased Sorley's cottage for three months—'

'There's no point in me staying longer!' he flared, only to groan inwardly when he saw her flinch. He'd meant simply that he didn't want to prolong the pain of the inevitable parting, but perhaps it was better if she misunderstood. 'Jess…Jess, I like you a lot.' Hell, that had to be the biggest understatement of the year, but to tell her he loved her, then walk away… 'I can't stay here. Greensay—it's not for me.'

'I see,' she said, her voice empty of all emotion.

'Jess—'

'You'd better go. Fred will be getting anxious.'

He nodded and strode to the door, but when he turned and glanced over his shoulder she was still standing in the centre of the room, and he knew the memory of her white, stricken face was going to haunt him for ever.

CHAPTER NINE

'WOWEE, I thought he was one good-looking man with his beard, but without it...' Cath's eyes followed Ezra appreciatively as strode off in the direction of his consulting room with Mrs Cuthbert. 'Like I said, wowee!'

'I preferred him with it,' Tracy said critically. 'I thought it made him look more romantic, mysterious.'

'Yes, but I bet it was hell of a scratchy when he kissed you.' Cath chuckled. 'I wonder what made him decide to shave it off?'

'I've no idea,' Jess replied, suddenly realising that both women were gazing at her expectantly. 'Perhaps it was his idea of a farewell gesture to Greensay.'

A frown creased Cath's forehead as Tracy bustled off to answer the phone. 'He's still leaving, then?'

'Of course. Dr Walton's arriving on Saturday afternoon so there's no need for him to stay on. Look, Cath, he's got every right to cut short his holiday if he wants to,' she added quickly when Cath said nothing. 'Just because he took Sorley McBain's holiday cottage for three months, it doesn't mean he has to stay for three months!'

'Did I say anything?' the receptionist protested. 'Did I?'

She didn't need to, Jess thought miserably as the postman shouldered open the surgery door and Cath hurried forward to relieve him of his pile of letters and circulars. The sympathy in her receptionist's eyes had been all too obvious, and the last thing she wanted was sympathy. Not when she was already so deeply embarrassed that she just wanted to crawl into a hole and stay there until Ezra left.

'I like you,' he'd said last night. 'There's no point in me staying longer,' he'd said, and not even her suggestion of

a brief affair—oh, how it made her cringe now just to remember it—had been enough to tempt him.

If only today was Saturday instead of Wednesday. How
was she going to get through the next few days when breakfast this morning had been a nightmare of stilted conversation and hastily averted glances, and the journey down to
the surgery in his car had been worse?

They'd talked about the weather. OK, so it was a dreadful morning—the wind coming in great gusts across the sea,
sending huge waves crashing against the harbour wall—but
the *weather*? Last night they would have made love if Fred
hadn't phoned, and now they were both so deeply embarrassed they were reduced to talking about the weather.

'Jess, it's the infirmary,' Tracy said, cradling the phone
against her chest. 'Colin McPhail didn't turn up for his
appointment with the orthopaedic surgeon yesterday, and
they want to know if he still wants to discuss a possible
hip replacement op.'

Jess sighed. She'd warned Ezra that Colin wouldn't go,
but he hadn't listened. She supposed she'd better check
with him, ask if he wanted to have another shot at per-
suading Colin... Except, of course, that he wouldn't. He
was leaving. Why, oh, why did she seem to have such
difficulty in remembering he was leaving?

'Ask them to make him another appointment,' she said
with an effort, reaching for her next patient's file, only to
pause as her eye fell on the one on top of Ezra's pile.
'Tracy, you've got Denise Fullarton's folder out.'

'I know.'

'But Denise is having home visits at the moment—'

'Not this morning I'm not.'

Jess gasped as she turned and saw Denise Fullarton smiling at her. 'Denise, are you bleeding, feeling ill?'

'I'm fine,' she interrupted. 'It's just... You see, I'm going to be twelve weeks pregnant on Sunday, and Dr Dunbar
is leaving on Saturday, and I want him to put the stitch in
my cervix before he goes.'

Denise's husband, Alec, was sitting in the waiting room, pretending to read a magazine, and Jess didn't know which of the couple she wanted to strangle first—him or Denise.

'I could have done it for you on Sunday,' she said tightly. 'I could have asked my new locum to drive me to your house.'

'I want Dr Dunbar to do it. I know this is going to sound silly but...' She coloured slightly. 'Somehow I just know if he does it, everything will be all right.'

'But—'

'Denise, what's wrong?' Ezra exclaimed, coming to a dead halt in the doorway to the consulting room. 'Are you bleeding?'

'No, she's not,' Jess interrupted flatly. 'She's here because she wants you to put a stitch in her cervix. She won't be twelve weeks pregnant until Sunday, you see,' she continued as Ezra gazed at her, bewildered, 'and she's got it into her head that if you do it the baby will be fine.'

'Please, don't be cross with me,' Denise said softly, seeing Ezra's face instantly mirror Jess's dismay. 'I know it sounds stupid—irrational—but I can't help the way I feel.'

Ezra glanced across at Jess, and she shrugged impotently. There was nothing she could say. There was plenty she *wanted* to say, but yelling at Denise wasn't going to do her, or her unborn baby, any good.

'Cath, would you take Denise through to the treatment room and get her ready for me?' Ezra asked, but the minute Denise had gone he angrily turned to Jess. 'What the hell was she thinking of, endangering herself and the baby like this?'

'You heard her—she wanted you.'

'That's just plain ridiculous,' he fumed. 'One doctor is pretty much like another...'

'Actually, no, they're not,' she said slowly. 'Gaining a patient's complete trust is a gift—a talent. It's ironic, really.' She laughed. A small, tight, strained, little laugh.

'You hate even the idea of being a GP, and yet you'd make a damn good one.'

'Jess…'

His eyes were dark, liquid, and her heart twisted inside her. She was going to burst into tears. She knew without a shadow of a doubt that if she didn't get away from him she was going to burst into tears, and quickly she glanced down at the folder in her hand. 'I'm ready for you now, Mrs Young.'

She quite patently wasn't, Ezra thought as he stared after her, and it was all his fault.

Hell, he wished last night had never happened. He'd spent the last five weeks trying to ensure that nothing like last night *could* ever happen, but…

It had been the way she'd looked at him, the little gasp she'd given when she'd seen him without his beard, the throaty chuckle. And before he'd realised it, he'd been kissing her, holding her, touching her, and if Fred Graham hadn't phoned, he would have made love to her.

He still wanted to—desperately—but to make love to her then leave…

If only he'd met her two years ago. Two years ago he'd had a career, a future, a name that had meant something in the medical world.

She would probably have disliked him intensely, he suddenly realised. The Ezra Dunbar of today was nothing like the Ezra Dunbar of two years ago. The old Ezra had been rude, arrogant and overbearing. He could still be all three, but living on Greensay had mellowed him. Falling in love with Jess had changed him completely.

Jess had said it was ironic that though he didn't want to be a GP he'd actually make a very good one. Well, there was another irony she knew nothing about. When he could have offered her so much more, she probably wouldn't have given him a second glance, but now that he had nothing to offer her he couldn't—wouldn't—offer just himself.

'Denise is ready for you now, Ezra,' Cath called, and he nodded, and slowly followed her into the treatment room.

'Now, you're to go straight home and into bed, Denise—'

'Jess, Dr Dunbar has already told me that ten million times.' Denise smiled.

'OK, so ten million and one won't hurt,' Jess said. 'How do you feel?'

'Sore,' Denise admitted. 'Sore, and relieved, and hopeful, and— Oh, Jess, I wish Dr Dunbar wasn't leaving. I've kept hoping and praying he might change his mind.'

'Denise, the island doesn't need two doctors.'

'Alec says it does. He says you need someone to help you.'

'Part time perhaps, but Dr Dunbar has his future to think of, and working here part time isn't his future.'

'I guess not,' Denise sighed. 'It's just—well, he's pretty special, isn't he?'

Yes, Ezra was special, Jess thought as she watched Alec help his wife out to their car, but he didn't want her, and she would just have to accept it.

And she would. People didn't die when relationships didn't work out. They might be a bit bruised by the experience, but they didn't die. When Ezra left on Saturday she would get on with her life, and eventually she would forget him. People said you could forget almost anything in time.

'You're looking a bit glum, Brian,' she commented as she went back to the reception desk to collect her next patient's file. 'Something wrong?'

He grimaced. 'Dr Dunbar's just told me it looks as though I'm going to have to be on this allopurinol stuff for my gout for the rest of my life. The level of uric acid in my blood test was high again, and I've not been cheating with my diet—not even a little bit.'

'I'm afraid it sounds like you're one of the unlucky ones,' she commiserated. 'Allopurinol *can* get rid of gout completely, but in some cases it doesn't and those people are always prone to fresh outbreaks.'

'That's what Dr Dunbar said.' He sighed. 'I can't say I like the idea of being on a drug for the rest of my life but, according to Dr Dunbar, there's no alternative. And I'm going to have to have blood tests all the time, too, to see whether the dosage needs altering.'

'Hey, look on the bright side, Brian.' She smiled. 'At least the allopurinol will mean no more agonising pain.'

'I suppose so,' he murmured, then brightened. 'Dr Dunbar told me he's leaving on Saturday.'

'That's right,' she said noncommittally.

'I'll be sorry to see him go,' Brian continued. 'He seems a good doctor and a decent enough bloke, though I have to say I didn't much like the idea of him living with you.'

'He had to live with me, Brian, or I would never have been able to cover any night calls.'

'Oh, I know that.' His plump face suddenly crimsoned with consternation. 'I hope you don't think I was implying...I mean, I wasn't suggesting...'

'I know you weren't,' Jess said soothingly. 'Dr Dunbar and I had a purely professional arrangement, just as Dr Walton and I will have.'

'He's going to be living with you now?'

His voice had come out in a squeak and a smile tugged at her lips. 'I expect Wattie Hope will say I've become quite the scarlet woman.'

'Let him try saying anything in my hearing,' he exclaimed, his plump jowls quivering with indignation. 'I'm not a violent man, but—'

'I think you're a lovely man,' she said gently. 'And one day I hope you'll meet someone who is truly worthy of you. Someone who can give you as much happiness as Leanne did.'

He stared at her silently for a moment, then he bit his lip. 'But it's not going to be you—that's what you're saying, isn't it? It's OK, Jess,' he continued, as she put out her hand to him. 'I guess I sort of knew, deep down, that you and I would never… But I kind of hoped, you know— as you do…'

'Brian, I'm sorry.'

'So am I. No—enough said,' he insisted when she tried to interrupt. 'I'll never mention it again, and I just hope, well, I hope we can still be friends.'

She smiled. 'Of course we can. In fact…' She leant forward and kissed him. 'I hope we'll always be the very best of friends.'

'Dr Arden.'

She glanced over her shoulder to see Ezra at the reception desk. 'Something you want?'

You, he thought. I want you. 'Tracy's given me a list of home visits for this afternoon, and I wondered if there was anyone else you wanted to add.'

She smiled a farewell at Brian, took the sheet of paper Ezra was holding out to her and scanned it quickly. 'That seems to be everybody. Was there something else?' she added, seeing indecision in his face as she handed the list back to him and he pushed it into his top pocket.

'No.' He reached for his bag, then paused. 'Yes, dammit, there is. If you marry Brian Guthrie you're out of your mind.'

She could have told him that she had absolutely no intention of marrying the farmer, but the condemnation she could hear in his voice had got under her skin.

'I don't think my private life is any of your business, do you?' she said tightly, hitching her crutches up under her arms.

'Look, I know he's reputed to be filthy rich—'

'You think I'd marry a man simply because he was *rich*!' she gasped in disbelief.

'Some women would.'

'I am *not* some women, Ezra.'

'No, I know you're not, but—'

'Shouldn't you be starting your home visits?' she pointed out icily as the surgery phone began to ring.

'Yes, but Brian Guthrie, Jess—'

'Like I said, what I do—or don't do—is none of your business, is it?' she snapped.

'Jess…'

'What is it, Tracy?' she interrupted, suddenly noticing that the girl was clutching the side of the desk convulsively and all colour had drained from her face.

'Danny… It's Danny.'

'What about him?' Jess demanded. 'Tracy, has he had an accident?'

'He…the harbour master said Danny was unloading fish from *The Aurora*, and he slipped, and…' A sob broke from the teenager. 'He's been crushed between two fishing boats, and they've taken him to the Sinclair Memorial.'

Jess was already making for the door with Ezra close behind when she suddenly realised that Tracy was pulling on her coat. 'Tracy, you can't come with us. Cath's not back from the post office yet—'

'I'm coming, and if you won't take me I'll walk to the Sinclair Memorial,' the girl replied determinedly.

'And leave Reception unattended?' Ezra exclaimed. 'Leave the phones unanswered if we get another emergency?'

Tears filled Tracy's eyes. 'But Danny… I've been so horrible to him recently. The things I've said…'

'Tracy, I know how you feel—believe me, I do,' Jess declared, her heart going out to the girl, 'but you *must* stay here until Cath gets back. Surely you can see that?'

For one awful moment she thought Tracy was going to argue with her, and the last thing she needed right now was an argument when time was of the essence, then the teenager nodded tearfully. 'You'll phone me? If Danny… If he… You'll phone me?'

'There'll be no need—I'm sure there won't,' Jess said

reassuringly, but when she accompanied Ezra out to his car her heart sank.

The weather was even worse now than it had been earlier in the day. The wind had risen to storm force, bringing with it driving sleet, and if Danny's injuries were as bad as they sounded he was in big trouble. The air ambulance would never be able to land in such a gale, and to subject Danny to a long voyage by lifeboat didn't even bear thinking about.

'OK, do you want the good news or the bad first?' Bev asked as soon as Jess and Ezra arrived at the hospital.

'Some good news would be nice,' Jess replied with feeling.

'He's fractured both his right and left femurs, four of his ribs are fractured and his left cheekbone's shattered.'

'That's the good news?' Jess said faintly.

'His right lung's collapsed, Jess, and the lifeboat can't get here for at least an hour and a half.'

An hour and a half. And then it would take another hour and a half for the lifeboat to return to the mainland, followed by a journey by road ambulance to the nearest hospital with A and E facilities. Danny would assuredly die before he reached help.

'What about the air ambulance?' Jess said desperately, although she already knew the answer.

'Will called them immediately after he spoke to the lifeboat station, but...' Bev shook her head. 'They can't risk putting a plane or a helicopter in the air until this gale dies down.'

'Then...?'

Bev nodded. 'Jess, you'll have to operate and stabilise him.'

An icy chill of fear crept round Jess's heart as she stared at the radiographer. She'd done part of the surgery course at med school, and had carried out many minor operations, but to do something as big as this on her own... Ezra could do it. He had the skill. Or at least he used to.

Ezra must have realised what she was thinking because he immediately shook his head. 'No, Jess. You know I can't.'

'Could you do it, Ezra?' Bev demanded, her eyes swivelling round to him. 'I heard about the wonderful job you did on Simon Ralston's hand—'

'Bev, I haven't operated on anyone for over a year.'

'But surely it's something you never forget—like riding a bike?' she protested. 'If you can do it—'

'I *can't!*' he exclaimed. 'Tell her, Jess. Tell her I *can't!*'

He began striding away, and Jess hopped awkwardly after him.

'Ezra—'

'Jess, don't you think I'd do it if I could?' he said harshly, his face haggard, pain-filled. 'I don't want him to die, but—'

'Would you…would you at least come into the operating theatre with me? I'm not asking you to operate,' she continued, as he thrust his fingers through his hair. She saw they were shaking. 'All I'm asking is if you'll be there beside me—perhaps give me your advice. Ezra, I can't do this by myself. I *need* you.'

Simply the thought of stepping into an operating theatre again was enough to make him feel physically sick, but as he stared down at her, saw the fear in her eyes, he knew he couldn't leave her to face this alone, not Jess.

'What sort of surgical equipment do you have?' he asked.

'The best money can buy.' His eyebrows rose, and she managed a smile. 'Our previous resident surgeon was determined Greensay was going to be prepared for anything.'

Except for not having a surgeon who could actually perform major operations, she thought, and knew Ezra was thinking the same.

'What about theatre staff?' he said tersely.

Cath had been a theatre sister for ten years before she'd

given it up to work at the health centre, but there was no way she could ask her to help, not in the circumstances.

'Will, of course,' she replied. 'Fiona has theatre experience, as do Jilly Thompson and Madge Greenwood.'

'Blood supplies?'

'Luckily Danny's type O, and we always carry a full supply of it because it's the universal donor which we can give to anyone.' He said nothing, and she stared up at him pleadingly. 'Ezra, I wouldn't ask you to do this unless I was desperate. You do know that, don't you?'

His eyes met hers for a long moment, then he swallowed—hard. 'Where do we scrub up?'

'Through here,' she replied, turning as quickly as she could in case he changed his mind.

It will be all right, she told herself when they went into the changing cubicles and put on their theatre scrubs. It will be all right, she kept repeating in the vain hope that if she said it often enough she might make it true.

'I'll have to perform a pneumothorax for his collapsed lung, won't I?' she said when they began to scrub up.

'Yes.'

'I did one once when I was training. I just hope I remember the drill.'

'Yes.'

'My major worry is that he might be bleeding internally,' she continued doggedly, shooting him a quick sidelong glance. 'When he was crushed between the two boats, he could have ruptured some internal organs.'

'Yes.'

Oh, God, it wasn't going to be all right. Ezra looked awful. Drained of all colour, tiny beads of sweat on his forehead. What was she going to do if he fainted? She needed him, and if he fainted...

'Tracy told me what happened,' a familiar voice suddenly said. 'Would one slightly rusty ex-theatre sister be of any use to you?'

Jess turned to see Cath standing in the doorway of the scrub room and let out a sigh of relief. 'You bet she would.'

'Cath, you can't be serious,' Ezra said in amazement, seeing her reach for a set of theatre scrubs. 'You underwent surgery yourself only two days ago!'

'A needle aspiration,' she said dismissively. 'And this is an emergency. At times like this we all rally round.'

And they did, Ezra realised, as Cath disappeared into one of the changing cubicles. They were incredible. Jess, Cath, the staff at the Sinclair Memorial, but especially Jess. Her leg was fractured in two places, she could barely stand without crutches and yet she was willing to operate, to do something she'd only done once before. Only he was useless. Only he would be a spectator—and an unwilling one at that.

'I don't much like the sound of his heart,' Will commented when they joined him in the operating theatre. 'The beats are far too close together.'

They were.

Tachycardia, for sure, Jess thought grimly. Danny had lost so much blood that his heart was needing to beat faster and faster in order to get what little blood he had left to his brain. And it shouldn't be happening. Not when the blood transfusion bags were up and running.

'IV's running wide open,' Cath declared. 'BP 60 over 40. No breath sounds on the left side.'

First things first, Jess told herself. Concentrate on his lung first. Danny's trachea was shifting further and further to the left, which meant that air was seeping into his chest, creating a large bubble of air which was compressing his collapsed lung. His aorta, as well as his heart, was being squashed by the increasing air in his chest, and he'd have a heart attack if she didn't relieve the pressure.

Quickly she stabbed a needle into his chest, then took the scalpel Cath was already holding out to her.

'How big should I make the incision, Ezra?' He didn't reply, and she glanced across at him. He was holding onto the edge of the operating table as though his very life depended on it. 'Ezra, the incision—how big should it be?'

He swallowed behind his mask. 'Make it…make it as small as you can. But remember you'll have to go right down into the lining of his lung, and when you ease the chest tube in, do it gently.'

Jess nodded. A trickle of sweat ran down her back as she made the incision. The chest tube next, she told herself as Cath held it out to her. Gently, Ezra had said. Ease it in gently. Almost there. She was sure it was almost there.

'Cath…'

'Chest tube hooked up, suction on,' she replied, and under Jess's thankful gaze Danny's lung gradually began to reinflate.

'BP now, Fiona?'

'Still 60 over 40.'

It should be going up, not remaining static. Why wasn't it going up? Had she done something wrong?

'Ezra…'

'No pulse, Jess!' Will suddenly yelled. 'We've got no pulse!'

Jess's eyes flew to Ezra's. The pericardium—the sac round Danny's heart—must be filling with fluid.

'A thoracotomy—you have to do a thoracotomy!' he exclaimed.

'I can't do that!' she protested. 'I'm not a surgeon!'

'Make a ten-inch horizontal incision across his breastbone right down to his ribs,' he ordered.

'But—'

'*Do it*, Jess!'

With trembling fingers, she did. She sliced down through Danny's chest. She saw his ribs, and his heart beneath them, but when Cath held out the large metal rib-spreader to her, she shook her head. 'I can't—I *can't*!'

'Jess, if you don't, he'll die for sure,' Cath said quickly.

She knew he would, but… Reluctantly, she took the

metal rib-spreader and closed her eyes. Oh, God, help me, she prayed. Please, God, please, God, help me.

And He did. The spreader was suddenly whisked out of her hands, and when she opened her eyes Ezra was holding it.

Without a word he inserted the metal instrument between two of Danny's ribs and spread them wide enough apart to get his hands into the chest cavity.

'Clamp, Cath!'

Obediently she handed him one, and swiftly he placed it on the lower portion of Danny's aorta so that what little blood there was in Danny's body would all be directed towards his brain to keep it alive. Then deftly he placed his hands round Danny's heart and swung it to the left.

'BP falling!' Fiona called out tensely.

It was, and they could all see why. When Danny had been crushed between the two boats, not only had four of his ribs been fractured but something had pierced his chest, ripping a hole in his heart.

'Finger, Jess—push your finger into the hole!' Ezra ordered. Obediently she did as he asked, and the flow of blood stopped instantly. 'Cath, sutures, needle, forceps.'

She passed them over to him, and with a speed Jess could only marvel at he inserted three large sutures into Danny's heart.

'BP still 60 over 40,' Fiona announced.

Ezra nodded, and slowly released the clamp he had inserted in Danny's aorta. Would the stitches hold? They all held their breath and waited.

'BP now, Fiona?' Ezra asked.

'Eighty over 60. Ninety over 70. One hundred over 80.'

The stitches were holding. Danny's blood pressure wasn't great, but they'd stabilised him, and a collective sigh of relief went up.

'I can manage here now, Jess,' Ezra said, seeing her slump slightly against the operating table. 'Your leg must be giving you hell.' It was, but she didn't want to leave, and he must have seen it in her eyes because he added softly, 'It's OK. I don't need you any more.'

No, he didn't need her any more, she thought sadly as she made her way into the changing room. She needed him—she loved him—but he didn't need her. He never had. She'd coaxed—blackmailed—him into medicine again, but now his confidence had returned he could go back to his world. And it was a world where she didn't belong.

'That has to be the most amazing piece of surgery I've ever seen,' Bev enthused as she joined Jess in the scrub room. 'The man's incredible!'

'I know,' Jess replied, managing to smile.

'And to think Will actually suggested he should apply for the post of surgeon at the Sinclair.' Bev shook her head in disbelief. 'No wonder he turned it down. Lord, if I had even half his ability I wouldn't want to be stuck on Greensay, operating on warts and verrucas.'

'No,' Jess murmured.

'I'd better phone Tracy,' the radiographer continued. 'She's been telephoning every ten minutes to see what's happening. I know Danny's not out of the woods yet, but at least Ezra's put him on the road to recovery. Talk of the devil,' she added with a beaming smile, as the door to the scrub room opened and Ezra appeared with Cath. 'Ezra Dunbar, you're a lifesaver!'

He certainly was, Jess thought as the two women showered him with praise. How could she ever have thought he'd be happy living on Greensay, working as a GP? This was where he belonged. In an operating theatre, performing major surgery, saving lives with his skill.

'You must be pleased,' she said when Bev had left to phone Tracy and Cath had hurried back to check on Danny.

'*Pleased?* Oh, Jess, you don't know what it means to me to be able to operate again,' he gasped, his face alight with relief and pleasure. 'To pick up a scalpel and not fall apart. It's the most wonderful feeling in the world!'

Her smile became a little crooked, a little uneven. She

would have said that being in love was the most wonderful feeling in the world but, then, she was only Jess Arden, GP, not Ezra Dunbar, surgeon.

'What do you want to do about the lifeboat?' she asked. 'Should we tell them to keep coming, or…?'

'Danny's stabilised for the moment,' he replied, 'and I really don't want him moved—at least not for the next twelve hours—unless it's absolutely necessary. I think he should stay here until the weather is calm enough for a helicopter to land.'

She nodded. 'You're the boss.'

He laughed. 'Lord, but I didn't think I'd ever hear any-one say that to me again! And you were amazing, Jess,' he continued, peeling off his surgical gloves and binning them. 'For someone who was never trained to be a surgeon, you did really well.'

'Thank you.'

'Cath was great, too,' he enthused. 'Helping out when she's got all this worry on her mind. She's some lady.'

'I know.'

A slight frown pleated his forehead and he gazed at her searchingly. 'Are you OK?'

'A bit tired, that's all,' she murmured, avoiding his eyes. 'I'm just glad I'm not a surgeon. I don't think I could stand that sort of pressure, day after day.'

'Jess, I have an idea. I was going to wait until later—tell you about it later—but…' He grinned. 'Oh, what the hell. I'll tell you now.'

'Sounds a bit ominous,' she replied, forcing an answer-ing smile to her own lips. 'What do you want to tell me?'

'Not tell so much as suggest,' he said. 'Jess, the Sinclair Memorial needs a qualified surgeon but not all the time. You need a GP but only a part-time one.' He cleared his throat. 'Now that I can operate again, what would you say to me applying for the post at the hospital and helping you in the practice as well?'

Twenty-four hours ago it would have been exactly what she'd have wanted him to say, but now...

'What about your career?'

'I could have a career here,' he said. 'You said once that you thought I'd make a very good GP.'

'That was before I saw you operate.'

'Yes, but I could operate here.'

'On what?' she asked. 'OK, perhaps once in a while you might get something really stretching, but for most of the time the operations you'd perform would be ordinary, mundane.'

'I wouldn't care,' he protested.

'Maybe not at first,' she murmured. Lord, what am I doing? she wondered as he stared at her silently. I'm talking him out of my life and I don't want him to leave, but if he stayed, grew embittered at the waste of his talent... Better for him to leave now. Better for him to go before he became as necessary to her as the air she breathed. 'Ezra, you're a surgeon at heart. This afternoon must have proved that to you.'

'But—'

'Once you're back on the mainland you'll thank me for what I'm doing,' she said, forcing a smile to her lips. 'Being a part-time surgeon and a part-time GP—it isn't for you, Ezra. There's nothing on this island for you.'

He'd hoped there was. He'd very much hoped that Jess might feel the same way about him as he did about her, but she obviously didn't.

'You're saying I should leave,' he said with a painful attempt at a smile. 'That you don't want me to stay.'

'That's what I'm saying, Ezra,' she said, feeling her heart twist and contract within her. 'I don't want you to stay.'

CHAPTER TEN

'EZRA wants to stay on Greensay.'

Jess put the magazines she'd brought for Mairi down on her bedside cabinet. 'He told you that, did he?'

'Not in so many words, but I've got eyes and ears, and I know he wants to stay.'

'He might think he does,' Jess said, 'but the novelty of living on an island—being a part-time GP and surgeon here—would soon wear off.'

Mairi's lips set into a thin line of disapproval. 'He's a grown man, Jess. Don't you think he should be allowed to find out for himself if he's made a mistake, rather than you giving him his marching orders?'

'I haven't!' she protested, and saw Mairi's eyebrows rise.

'No? He's offered to work part-time with you, and you've turned him down. You've even managed to dissuade him from applying for the post here at the hospital. Sounds to me like you've given him his marching orders.'

Jess bit her lip. 'I just…Mairi, I want him to be happy. I don't want him to become resentful or bitter, and that's what I think will happen if he stays here.'

'Oh, lass, lass, can't you see *you're* the only one who can make him happy? *You're* the reason he wants to stay. He wants to be near *you*.'

A wry smile crossed Jess's face, and she picked up the glass of water on Mairi's bedside cabinet and sniffed it. 'What's Fiona being putting in this?'

'Jess, he's in love with you—'

'No, he's not. Look, I think I know him better than you do,' she continued when Mairi tried to interrupt. 'So let's just leave it, OK?'

Mairi opened her mouth, closed it again and shook her head. 'All right, I'll leave it, but I hope you know what you're doing.'

'I do.' Jess nodded. And she did, she decided when she finally left Mairi's room, and made her way along to Reception to meet Ezra.

If Ezra left today there was a chance her heart would eventually heal, but if he stayed on… To watch him grow bored with the island, bored with his work, resentful of everyone and everything on it? It was too high a price to pay, much too high.

'How's Mairi?' Ezra asked when he saw her.

'A bit brighter, I think,' she responded. 'And Danny?'

'Amazing, considering he had his accident only a few days ago. Are you still having him airlifted to the mainland tomorrow?' he continued as they walked towards his car.

'It seems the best thing to do under the circumstances. You won't be here, and if he had a relapse it would be a nightmare, trying to split myself between him and the practice.'

Not if you'd let me stay on, he longed to shout as they drove down to the health centre. OK, so you don't love me, and maybe you never will, but I still want to stay here, and it's not just because I want to be near you. I'm happy here. For the first time in my life I'm happy.

But he didn't say any of that. Instead, he said, 'Does everyone know there won't be any home visits this afternoon?'

'They should do. I got Tracy to put a notice up outside the surgery and in Nazir's shop. I also told Wattie Hope.'

Ezra's lips curved. 'Then I think we can safely say that everyone on the island knows.'

'I would say so.' She chuckled.

'What about your tuberculin testing clinic tonight?' he asked.

'I've cancelled it. It seemed a bit much to expect Dr Walton to work on his first night here.'

'Perhaps.' Ezra frowned. 'But won't that mean all the tests won't be completed now until the end of next week?'

'Yes, but at least none of the tests we've already taken has proved positive,' she argued back. 'Look, I've got everything under control, Ezra,' she continued, seeing his frown deepen. 'There's no need for you to worry, or feel you're leaving me in the lurch. Dr Walton's arriving this afternoon to take your place, so everything's fine.'

In other words, you don't need me, he thought sadly as they arrived at the health centre. He might need her, but she didn't need him.

'How's Danny this morning?' Tracy asked as soon as she saw them.

'Doing very well, apparently.' Jess smiled.

'I was hoping to visit him this morning,' Tracy said, her face distinctly truculent. 'This was supposed to be my Saturday off, not Cath's.'

Jess's smile didn't waver for an instant. 'She had some urgent business to attend to on the mainland.'

'A bit sudden, wasn't it?'

'Urgent business usually is,' Jess observed evenly. 'Has my first patient arrived yet?' she added before the girl could delve any deeper into Cath's whereabouts.

'It's Hildy Wells.'

And Hildy looked every bit as truculent as Tracy, Jess thought with a deep sigh as she ushered her through to her consulting room.

'I really don't see why you couldn't simply have given me a repeat prescription for my hormone replacement therapy, Doctor,' she grumbled. 'I'd hoped to go to the mainland this weekend to do some shopping, but Tracy said you wouldn't give me a prescription unless you saw me.'

'Hildy, I'm not happy about your fluctuating blood pressure or all these extra migraine attacks you've been having. Now, if you could just take off your coat and roll up your sleeve for me, I'll check your blood pressure.'

'It's always been erratic, you know that, Doctor,' Hildy

protested, reluctantly taking off her coat. 'And Sharps are having their big winter furniture sale today. In fact, I wouldn't be at all surprised if that's where Cath's gone.'

'Really,' Jess murmured noncommittally, keeping her eyes fixed on the blood-pressure gauge.

Hildy nodded. 'Wattie said he happened to notice her getting on the seven o'clock ferry this morning.'

Didn't the man ever sleep? Obviously not.

'As I suspected, your blood pressure's up again,' Jess said. 'Have you kept a diary of your migraine attacks—managed to establish any kind of pattern to them?'

'I seem to get more of them when I change from the estragest patches to the Estraderm ones.'

'Which would suggest your migraine attacks are hormonal,' Jess observed. 'What I'd like to do is try you on a different type of HRT, pills instead of patches, to see if that will regulate your blood pressure and put a stop to all your extra migraine attacks.'

'Just so long as you don't take me off it all together,' Hildy said, rolling down her sleeve. 'I was so weepy and bad-tempered before, and I don't want to go back to that again.'

'There's lots of things we can try,' Jess said reassuringly. 'It's just a question of getting the right combination for you.'

'Speaking of combinations,' Hildy continued as Jess wrote out her prescription, 'Wattie said that when he saw Cath getting on the ferry this morning he was sure her husband and daughter were with her.'

'Did he?' Jess murmured.

'I told him he must need his eyes tested because I was sure Cath told me Peter wasn't due back from the Gulf until March.'

'I'm afraid I wouldn't know,' Jess replied.

'But surely—working for you—she must have said—'

'I'd like to see you again in a month to check your blood pressure,' Jess declared, determinedly leading the way out of her consulting room. 'But if you find you're getting even more migraines, come back to me at once.'

That Hildy considered her a very poor source of information was plain, but there was no way Jess was going to discuss Cath's private business with anyone. And certainly not with someone who was second only to Wattie when it came to spreading gossip on the island.

Involuntarily her eyes went to the waiting-room clock. It was a little after ten. Cath would have arrived at the infirmary by now. She'd have filled in the consent form and changed into one of those awful theatre gowns that never had enough tapes down the back. And then she'd have to wait.

'She'll be OK, Jess,' Ezra said softly, noticing the direction of her gaze as he joined her at the reception desk. 'I've got a good feeling about this.'

'I wish I did,' she sighed. 'I wish she'd had the biopsy, and we knew what we were facing.'

'What time did the infirmary say they'd telephone to give us her results?' Ezra asked.

'Not until after three. Apparently they do all the tests, then double check them to make sure.'

'She'll be fine, Jess,' he insisted. 'I'm sure she will.'

'I hope so.' Quickly she lifted her next file, then hesitated. 'I've got Robb MacGregor next, but the results of his first jejunal biopsy suggest very strongly that he might have coeliac disease. As you were the one to spot it, would you like the pleasure of telling him?'

He grinned. 'I don't know whether I'd consider having coeliac disease a pleasure!'

'You would if you originally thought you had cancer.' She laughed, only for her laughter to die instantly as she suddenly remembered Cath.

'Jess, we're not going to know anything until this afternoon,' Ezra said gently. 'So, until then, try to put it out of your mind, hmm?'

There was such sympathy and understanding in his voice

that she had to swallow quickly. 'Would…would you like to see Robb?'

'If you don't mind?'

'Of course I don't,' she replied, handing him the folder, then selecting another one. 'Mrs Walker, I'm ready for you now.'

A heavily pregnant Beatrice Walker levered herself upright and Ezra sighed as he watched the two women leave the waiting room.

Jess looked so tired. Actually, he couldn't remember a day since he'd come to the island when she *hadn't* looked tired. And it wasn't simply because of her accident or her worry about Cath. Those dark shadows under her eyes had been there for a very long time.

Which was why he'd been so ecstatic when he'd completed Danny Hislop's operation. Not because it meant he could be a surgeon on the mainland again, but because he'd suddenly realised he could remain on Greensay. He could work part time at the Sinclair Memorial, and part time with Jess. He could stay here and be happy. He could stay with Jess.

And then, just when he'd thought everything he so desperately wanted had been within his grasp, she'd turned round and told him she didn't want him to stay.

Why had she kissed him so passionately if he meant nothing to her? She'd mumbled some rubbish after Danny's operation about his skill being wasted here, but surely she must know that he wouldn't consider it wasted? Here, he'd felt whole for the first time in his life. Complete. So why wouldn't she let him stay?

Because she doesn't love you, you idiot, his mind whispered. She's realised you're in love with her, and she's trying to let you down gently, and you're just too damned stupid to take the hint.

'I hope you've got some news for me, Doc,' Robb MacGregor said as he followed Ezra along to his consulting room. 'Because I've got to tell you, I'm just about at the end of my tether.'

So am I, Ezra thought as he explained to Robb that the results of his first test suggested he could well be suffering from coeliac disease.

'But I've eaten wheat for years, Doctor,' the builder protested. 'Surely, if I'd been allergic to it, it would have shown up when I was a child?'

'It's certainly more commonly found in children,' Ezra agreed, 'but we're increasingly finding it flaring up in adults.'

'But—'

'If you're going to ask me why, the simple answer is that nobody knows.' Ezra smiled. 'The good news, however, is that if your other tests prove you do have coeliac disease, it's very easy to treat. You simply stop eating gluten.'

'And then the rash—all my aches and pains—will simply disappear?' Robb exclaimed in disbelief.

'That's right.' Ezra nodded. 'All you'll have to do is cut out all foods that contain wheat, rye or barley, and your symptoms will disappear within days.'

'When will I know for certain if I have this disease?'

'It will probably take about three months to get a definite diagnosis. We can't do the three tests quickly, you see,' Ezra explained as Robb looked distinctly crestfallen. 'You have to have been on a gluten-free diet for a few weeks, then on a diet where the gluten has been reintroduced for a little while, or we wouldn't get a true assessment.'

'It's a pity you're leaving today, then, Doc,' Robb said. 'Because you'll never know if I do have coeliac disease, will you?'

No, he would never know, Ezra thought when Robb had left. Just as he'd never know if Denise Fullarton had carried her baby to term or lost this one, too. Or if Colin McPhail might one day agree to a hip replacement operation. And Cath…

His eyes went to his consulting-room clock. It was half past ten. She would be having her pre-med now in preparation for Theatre. Did she have breast cancer, or was it simply—as he prayed it was—a fibroadenoma? And if it wasn't...

He wanted to be there when Jess talked to Cath. He wanted to advise her, to help her, but this afternoon he was getting on the ferry, leaving.

And he didn't even know where he was going, he thought ruefully as morning surgery dragged by. Not back to London. The city held no attraction for him any more. Neither did he want to return to full-time surgery. Jess had suggested he could teach, but...

General practice. He would become a fully qualified GP. It would mean starting at the bottom again—working out his time as a locum at various practices—but he didn't care. Only as a GP would he have the human contact he knew he needed. And without Jess he was going to need a lot of human contact to get him through the rest of his life.

'Are you absolutely sure you don't want me to stay on for the rest of the afternoon?' Tracy asked when the last of their morning patients had gone. 'I know I was a bit grumpy earlier, but if you need me...'

'Don't be silly,' Jess said. 'You get off home. In fact, why don't you go and visit Danny?' she continued as the girl stared at her uncertainly. 'I'll mind the fort here. I've got masses of paperwork to do, and I may as well do it here rather than lug it all home.'

'If you're really sure?' Tracy said hesitantly.

'I'm sure,' Jess insisted.

The girl needed no second bidding. With a smile at Ezra she picked up her coat and was gone.

'I think I hear wedding bells in the near future for a certain young lady when a particular young man is fit enough to be discharged from hospital,' Ezra commented.

'I think I hear them, too.' Jess smiled. 'Look, you don't

have to hang about here,' she went on. 'Why don't you go back to the cottage, pack up all your things? Your ferry leaves at three forty-five.'

'I've already packed. I did it last night when you went to bed,' he added as her eyebrows rose in surprise. 'All my worldly possessions are now stowed in the boot of my car.'

'Yes, but—'

'I'd like to stick around. Hear what the infirmary has to say about Cath.'

He meant it. She knew that he did. And much as she didn't want to admit it, the thought of sitting alone in the surgery for the next two hours, waiting for the phone to ring, filled her with dread.

'Won't you get bored?' she asked, giving him one last chance to back out.

Ezra shook his head. 'It will give me an opportunity to bring all my files up to date.'

And so they worked silently together for the next two hours. Jess hadn't realised how time had passed until the surgery phone began to ring. Her eyes flew to the waiting room clock, then to Ezra.

'Do you want me to answer it?' he offered.

She shook her head. Since morning she'd been waiting for this phone call. Since morning she'd been praying, hoping, and now she would know. And something told her she wouldn't want to know.

'She's got breast cancer?' Ezra said when she finally put down the phone and sat staring at it.

'Yes.' There was nothing else Jess could say. Nothing else she could squeeze past the hard, cold lump in her throat.

'How…how extensive is it?' he asked.

'The lump was cancerous, as were some of the tissues in the muscles of her chest wall.'

He bit his lip. Breast cancer wasn't his speciality, but even he knew that wasn't good.

'OK, let's look at the options,' he declared, forcing himself into professional mode though it was the last thing he felt like doing at the moment. 'A lumpectomy would remove the affected lump and tissue, leaving her breast intact. I don't know the exact statistics but I believe the survival rates after such a procedure are very good.'

'Yes.'

'And even if the cancer has spread to her lymph glands, and her surgeon recommends a radical mastectomy, her chances of surviving are still very good.'

'I know.'

'Jess—'

'Why, Ezra?' she whispered, her voice breaking. 'I know there's no such thing as fairness with breast cancer—that as far as we know it's a lottery as to who will, and who won't, contract the disease—but Cath…'

'She'll get through this, Jess,' he insisted. 'OK, so she's got breast cancer, but once she's had surgery—'

'If she agrees to it.'

He stared at her strained, white face with dismay. Surely the receptionist wouldn't refuse? He wouldn't allow her to. 'I'll talk to her.'

'You won't be here.'

'I'll cancel my ferry ticket,' he said. 'Buy another one for later.'

'Ezra, you have to go some time, and I think it's better you go now rather than later, don't you?' She smiled. An uneven, crooked smile that tore at his heart. 'I'll manage. I managed on my own before. I can manage again.'

'Fine. Great. You can manage,' he retorted, his love for her making him angry. 'And for how long do you plan on *managing* on your own?'

'Dr Walton's going to be with me for the next eight weeks, and while he's here I'll advertise for a part-time partner.'

'And what if you don't get any applicants?' he protested.

'You said I would,' she pointed out. 'You said there must be lots of doctors wanting to escape from the rat race.'

'Yes, but—'

'It's not your problem, Ezra,' she said in a voice that told him the subject was well and truly closed. Quickly she reached for her coat, put her mobile phone in her pocket and hitched her crutches under her arms. 'Are you ready, then?'

'What for?' he demanded.

'Your ferry will be leaving in forty minutes, so we'd better get going or you'll miss it.'

'Look, you don't have to escort me off the island,' he flared. 'I *am* going, OK?'

A deep flush of colour crept across her white cheeks. 'I didn't mean… I wasn't implying… I just thought that as Dr Walton is arriving on the ferry, it would be a nice gesture if I was there to meet him.'

Ezra didn't give a damn if there was nobody there to meet Dr Walton. He didn't care if the man was still standing on the quayside in a week's time. 'Jess—'

'I don't want to be late, Ezra.'

He didn't want to go at all, he thought as he drove down to the harbour. Then tell her, his mind insisted, *tell her!*

But he knew that he wouldn't. To embarrass her with a declaration of love she couldn't return? Unconsciously he shook his head. He was going to be adult about this. He was going to simply shake her by the hand, say goodbye and then get on the boat, even though every part of him longed to take her back to her cottage and keep her there until she fell in love with him.

'I didn't know you were sailing this afternoon, Dr Arden,' the harbour master said when Ezra helped her out of his car onto the quayside.

'I'm not. Dr Dunbar is.'

'Oh, of course.' He nodded. 'This is your last day with us, isn't it, Doctor? Well, you've got a lovely day for your crossing.'

And it was lovely, Jess thought as she saw the ferry ploughing its way towards them through the white-capped sea. In the movies it always rained when the heroine was unhappy, but today the sun was shining, the sky was blue and everything should have been all right with the world. Except that it wasn't.

Lord, but she was going to miss him, but she was going to be adult about this. She was going to stand on the quay-side and wave goodbye. Later she would cry her eyes out, but not now. Now Ezra was never going to know that send-ing him away was the hardest thing she'd ever done, and that he was taking her heart with him.

'Are you sure you've got everything?' she forced herself to ask. 'All your clothes, your books, shoes?'

'I think so,' he replied, equally formally. 'If I've forgot-ten anything, it can't be very important.'

'No,' she murmured, and his throat tightened.

He couldn't leave like this. OK, so Jess would probably be deeply embarrassed if he told her he loved her, but he *had* to tell her.

'Jess—'

'Off on the ferry back to the mainland, are you, Dr Dunbar?'

Go away, Ezra thought grimly as he turned to see Wattie Hope beaming up at him. For God's sake, just go away. I'm leaving, and I want to tell Jess I love her. I know she's going to knock me back, but I want to remember everything about this moment—what she's wearing, how she looks, what she says—because this is the last time I'll ever see her, and these few precious minutes are going to have to last me a lifetime.

'Your new locum's arriving on the ferry, isn't he, Dr Arden?' Wattie continued, apparently oblivious to the daggers Ezra was shooting at him. 'Name of Walton, if I remember rightly?'

'Yes,' Jess replied.

Why couldn't he simply go away? The ferry had docked. They'd lowered the gangway and the car deck doors were being opened, and though these last few minutes with Ezra were tearing her heart apart she still wanted to share them with him alone.

'I don't see any sign of Cath Stewart,' Wattie observed, scanning the deck of the ferry. 'Do you think she's missed the boat?'

'Mrs Stewart's not due back on Greensay until Monday,' Jess said through gritted teeth.

'Really? So she's making a long weekend of it—she and her husband and daughter? It *was* her husband I saw with her this morning, wasn't it?'

'I've no idea, Wattie, and now if you'll excuse me—'

'Would you have any idea what this Dr Walton looks like?'

'No, she bloody well wouldn't!' Ezra retorted, so fiercely that Wattie stepped back a pace.

'Right... I see. Well, I think—I think I might just go and have a word with the harbour master,' he said.

'Don't let us keep you,' Ezra said grimly.

'No. Right, I'll see you later, then,' Wattie said, and beat a very hasty retreat.

'That's one person you certainly aren't going to miss,' Jess said with a small smile.

'No.' He cleared his throat. 'Jess—'

'You can drive your car on board now, Dr Dunbar,' one of the ferrymen called.

Quickly Ezra delved into his pocket and threw his car keys to him. 'Would you do it for me?'

The young man looked at Ezra's blue Mercedes, and his eyes lit up. 'You bet!'

But when Ezra turned quickly back to Jess she wasn't looking at him any more but at the gangway.

'Do you think that's him?' she said. 'Dr Walton?'

It had to be, he thought, his lip curling as he followed the direction of her gaze. Nobody else would arrive on Greensay wearing a grey pinstriped city suit and carrying an umbrella.

'He looks a complete prat,' he couldn't help saying.

'As long as he's a half-decent doctor, I don't care what he looks like,' she said.

'Jess—'

Hesitantly she held out her hand to him. 'Well, it's good-bye, then, Ezra.'

There was so much he wanted to say, so much he needed to say, but the only words he could force out of his mouth were, 'Take care of yourself, Jess.'

'You, too,' she replied.

'I've enjoyed my stay here,' he continued. 'Maybe… maybe some time I might come back for a holiday.'

He wouldn't—she knew he wouldn't—and he knew it, too.

'You'd better get on board,' she said. 'The ferry will be leaving soon.'

He put out his hand to her, and for one wonderful moment she thought he might kiss her, then suddenly he turned abruptly away and began walking towards the gang-way.

Part of her wanted to go after him—to tell him to stay—but she forced herself to stay where she was. It's for the best, Jess, she told herself. He would never be happy here. It's for the best, she kept repeating, and wished she could make herself believe it.

'Dr Arden?'

Blindly she turned to see the young man she'd noticed coming down the gangway gazing at her with a frown.

'Yes, I'm Dr Arden,' she said with an effort. 'You must be…'

'Phil Walton.' He gazed critically around him. 'I have to say the island looks a lot smaller than I thought.'

'You've only seen the harbour so far, Dr Walton.'

He didn't look convinced. 'Where's the harbour master's office?'

'The harbour master's office?' she repeated in confusion.

'My car.' He pointed to the white Peugeot on the quayside. 'It was damaged on the voyage over, and I know what insurance firms are like. Unless you report it immediately, they drag their heels about paying up.'

She gazed at the car, then back at him. 'I don't see any damage.'

'It's been scraped,' he protested, pointing to a minuscule scratch on the wing. 'I bought it only a month ago, and it's been scraped!'

She stared at him in disbelief. 'Dr Walton—'

She came to a halt as the air was suddenly shattered by the sound of a ship's horn. The ferry was leaving. While this stupid man had been complaining about nothing, the ferry had pulled away from the quayside.

Quickly she scanned the deck, looking for Ezra, but there was no sign of him. Had he gone below already? She'd thought—hoped—he might at least wave to her, but...

'The harbour master's office, Dr Arden?'

'It's over there, Dr Walton,' she snapped, pointing to the small hut at the end of the quayside.

He followed the direction of her hand, then grimaced. 'A hut. How quaint.'

He wasn't quaint, she thought as she watched the ferry sailing out of the harbour. He was going to drive her mad in a day, and because of him she hadn't even been able to wave goodbye to Ezra. He was gone, out of her life.

Miserably she turned away, unwilling to watch the ferry any longer, and gasped when she saw a familiar figure sitting on one of the capstans.

'Ezra, what happened? I saw you get on the ferry.'

'I got off again.'

'Did you forget something? You could have telephoned. I would have sent it on to you.'

'Jess, I'm not leaving. I've decided to apply for the post of surgeon at the Sinclair Memorial, and I don't care if it pays peanuts and I have to live in a caravan. I'm staying here.'

'You're...you're just nervous about the future,' she said

uncertainly. 'It's understandable, not having worked as a surgeon on the mainland for over a year, but once you're back in the swing of things—'

'I don't *want* to be back in the swing of things—can't you see that?' he said angrily. 'Jess, I'm thirty-four years old, and for the first time in my life I know what happiness is, and I don't want to lose it.'

'But your career...'

'I've had a career. I've had the admiration and the recognition it can bring, but I've never had a life.'

'But—'

'Jess, I want people to grieve for me when I'm gone. I want people to call me Ezra instead of Mr Dunbar. But the most important thing...' His eyes caught and held hers. 'The most important thing is I want you.'

'Me?' she said faintly.

'Jess, I'm in love with you. I think I've been in love with you ever since you hid my lunch in your medical bag.'

'But you can't be in love with me.'

'Will you stop telling me what I can or can't do?' he exclaimed. 'If I want to be in love with you, I *will* be in love with you. I'm not asking you to love me back. All I'm asking is to be allowed to stay here, and maybe...maybe in time you might fall in love with me.'

Tears clogged Jess's throat. 'Oh, Ezra...'

'I know Brian Guthrie has more money than I'll ever earn in a lifetime—'

'I've never been interested in money,' she said softly.

'And I know Fraser Kennedy is younger than me, better-looking—'

'He hasn't got a cleft chin or black hair.'

Hope flared in his eyes. Hope, and uncertainty, and longing. 'Are you saying...? Do you mean...?'

'Ezra, I love you, too,' she whispered. 'I think I've loved you since you told me I was the most stubbornly vexatious woman it had ever been your misfortune to meet, but are

you sure? You're throwing away so much. I don't want
you to look back on this moment and regret it—'

'Jess, I'm giving up nothing that's important to me. The
only thing—the *only* thing—that matters in my life is you.
I love you. And I want to marry you.'

A cry broke from her—a cry that was halfway between
a laugh and a sob—and before she knew it she was in his
arms and he was kissing her, holding her as though he
never wanted to let her go. And he didn't.

'Let's go home, Jess,' he murmured huskily. 'Let's go
home and pray the phone doesn't ring because I want to
show you just how much I love you.'

She nodded, then gasped as she suddenly remembered.
'But your car—all your things. They're on their way to the
mainland!'

'I'll phone the terminal—get them to send it back on
Monday's ferry. Jess, it doesn't matter,' he said as she continued to stare at him in dismay.

'But it's not just your car. What am I going to do about
Dr Walton? He's awful.'

'Can't you just send him back?'

She shook her head. 'If I send him back, I'll have to pay
hefty cancellation fees. The only way we can get rid of him
is if he resigns.'

A frown pleated Ezra's forehead, then a slow smile
spread across his face. 'Did you tell the agency he'd be
staying with you?'

She shook her head. 'I just said accommodation would
be available.'

'I understand Wattie occasionally rents out rooms in his
house.'

'Ezra, we couldn't…'

'You said he was awful, didn't you?'

'Yes, but—'

'I want you all to myself, Jess Arden,' he said, his face

alight with love. 'Today—tomorrow—for the rest of my life.'

And as he gathered her into his arms and kissed her again, Phil Walton was forgotten, and her only thoughts were about the new and wonderful future that lay ahead.

EPILOGUE

'JESS, if we don't hurry up we're going to be late.'

'I know.' Desperately she tugged at the zip on her skirt. Lord, it was tight. Only last month it had fitted perfectly, but now…

'Should we take both our mobiles?' Ezra asked, popping his head round the bedroom door, looking immaculate in a dark blue suit, white shirt and green silk tie.

'We'd better.' She nodded. 'That way, we'll have both the hospital and the surgery covered.' Quickly she slipped on the loose jacket that went with the skirt, adjusted her wide-brimmed straw hat and grimaced. 'I look like a mushroom.'

'You look lovely,' he exclaimed, and she shook her head.

'Ezra, you'd say I looked lovely if I was wearing a potato sack.'

'And you would,' he said, taking her in his arms. 'In fact, Mrs Dunbar, have I told you lately how much I love you?'

She chuckled. 'Only four times a day on average since we got married.'

'Four times?' he murmured. 'It's not enough—nowhere near enough.'

For a second she enjoyed the feel of his arms around her, but when she felt his fingers moving to the front of her blouse she shook her head. 'Ezra, we have to go. If we're late for baby Fullarton's christening, Denise will never forgive us.'

He sighed regretfully. 'I still don't know how she managed to talk us into being godparents.'

'By not taking no for an answer,' she said with a laugh as she led the way out of the cottage.

And Denise hadn't. Nothing they'd said had dissuaded her, and now the entire population was assembling at the small island church for the christening. In fact, the last time St Mary's had seen such a gathering had been exactly a year ago when Jess and Ezra had got married.

Jess's lips curved as she remembered. Ezra had wanted them to get married right away, and so had she, but once Mairi had heard the news, and then Cath, it had been taken out of their hands.

'Make it a June wedding,' Mairi had insisted. 'By June I won't be infectious any more, and I want to arrange everything.'

'June, most definitely,' Cath had agreed. 'Not July or August. I'm having my mastectomy at the end of April, then I'll have to start on the chemotherapy in July, and though I don't mind turning up for your wedding with one breast, I'm damned if I'm going to appear bald in your wedding pictures.'

So June it had been, and it had been a wonderful wedding. It had been a wonderful year.

It was a lovely christening, too, even though Ezra was none too happy when the minister declared that Denise and Alec's son would be henceforth known as Ezra Alec Fullarton.

'The poor little soul's going to hate me when he grows up,' he told Denise at the buffet lunch in the village hall afterwards. 'What were you thinking of—landing him with an old-fashioned name like mine?'

'There's nothing wrong with Ezra,' Denise said stoutly. 'And Alec and I felt we had to call him after you when we owe you so much.'

'You don't owe me anything,' Ezra protested. 'This pregnancy was simply meant to go full term this time, that's all.'

'You're never going to convince her, you know,' Jess

observed, as Denise bustled away with her son to have a few words with the minister.

'I guess not.' He smiled, then frowned slightly. 'You've been very quiet all afternoon. Anything wrong?'

She shook her head. 'I just can't believe we've been married for a whole year, that's all.'

'I can.'

'You mean it seems much longer?' she said uncertainly, and he reached for her hand and squeezed it.

'I mean that as soon as I met you I knew one lifetime was never going to be enough.'

Tears filled her eyes, and she rapidly blinked them away. 'No regrets, then?'

His grip on her hand tightened. 'Jess, I have you and two jobs that have given me more happiness and fulfilment than I could ever have thought possible. What more could I want?'

Hopefully, one more thing, she thought, taking a deep breath. 'Ezra, there's something I want to—'

'Don't you just love a christening?' Mairi Morrison beamed as she joined them at the buffet table. 'A christening or a wedding—both have me in floods of tears every time.'

'I hope that's not all you're going to eat, Mairi,' Brian Guthrie chastised, adding another two sandwiches and a vol-au-vent to her plate. 'You've got to build yourself up, you know. TB's a nasty thing, and though you're over it now, you're still far too thin.'

Ezra's jaw dropped as Brian solicitously shepherded Mairi away. 'Good grief, you don't think those two…?'

Jess chuckled. 'Maybe it's in the air. Us getting married, then Tracy and Danny. Maybe it's infectious.'

He grinned, then shook his head as she selected another salmon sandwich. 'I thought you said you were going on a diet?'

'Ezra, you should know by now I'm *always* going on a

diet.' She laughed. 'And anyway, I thought you said you liked my figure?'

He put his arm round her. 'I do. It's perfect. Every inch of it.'

'So you wouldn't mind if I added a few more?' she asked, and when he shook his head she cleared her throat. 'Good, because there's something I want to tell you—'

'Sorry to interrupt, Docs, and I know a christening's not the place to be talking business, but I wondered if you'd given any more thought to the plans I drew up for extending your cottage?' Robb MacGregor asked. 'Like I said at the time, you'll probably be thinking about starting a family yourselves soon, and a cottage with two bedrooms really isn't big enough.'

'We liked the plans,' Ezra replied, 'but we both think the quote you gave us was far too low.'

'You let me worry about the quote,' Robb said, reaching for a crab sandwich, only to put it down quickly when Ezra's eyebrows snapped together. 'Force of habit, Doc. Sometimes I forget about the gluten.'

'Not too often, I hope.' Ezra frowned, and the builder shook his head.

'No way. The last thing I want is to go back to feeling as wretched as I did a year ago before we knew I had coeliac disease. So, are we on for the extension, or what?'

'Most definitely on,' Jess said before Ezra could reply. 'In fact, the sooner the better.'

'I thought you said we should wait,' Ezra said curiously as the builder walked away. 'That it would cause too much upheaval?'

'I know I did but, you see—'

'Jess, you wouldn't happen to have seen the big silver cake knife?' Cath asked, looking distinctly harassed. 'Alec and Denise want to cut the cake, and I thought I put it—'

'It's in the kitchen, Mum,' her daughter Rebecca chipped in. 'You said it would be safer there with all these kids running about the place.'

'So I did.' Cath shook her head. 'Honestly, this is the last time I'm ever going to organise anything. I don't know whether I'm on my head or my heels.'

'And you're loving every minute of it,' her daughter said giggling, and Jess smiled as Rebecca and Cath headed off together towards the kitchen.

Cath's cancer had brought mother and daughter much closer together, and though it had been a rough year for Cath—undergoing a mastectomy, and then chemotherapy—her last scan had shown no recurrence of the cancer. Now she could begin considering the pros and cons of reconstructive surgery, but Jess knew that no matter what Cath decided she would be all right.

'OK. You can tell me now.'

She turned to see Ezra smiling down at her. 'Tell you what?'

'What you've been trying to tell me all afternoon, but keep getting interrupted.'

She stared up at him. She loved him so much, and though she was delighted with the news... 'It doesn't matter—it can wait.'

His grey eyes danced. 'If you're trying to pluck up the courage to tell me you dented the Mercedes last night when you were out on call, I know already.'

'It's not that. It's...' She glanced over her shoulder. It was too public here—much too public. 'Come outside for a minute.'

'Look, if it's about the fax machine, I know it was Tracy who jammed all the incoming mail,' Ezra said as he followed her out of the village hall. 'And, yes, it was a stupid thing to do, but we can't expect her to know as much as Cath did—'

'It's not Tracy. It's...' She coloured slightly. 'Do you remember when we talked about starting a family?'

He nodded. 'We decided we'd wait a couple of years.'

'I know we did, but...' Her colour deepened. 'How

would you feel about starting one a lot sooner than we planned? Like in six months?'

He stared at her silently for a second, then a smile curved his lips. A smile that grew and grew until his whole face lit up. 'Jess, do you mean…? Are you…are we…?'

She nodded. 'I don't know how it happened—'

Ezra threw back his head and laughed. 'And she calls herself a doctor. Oh, Jess, this is the icing on the cake—the cherry on top of the pie—all my birthdays in one!'

'You don't mind?' she said uncertainly. 'I know it isn't what we planned—'

'To hell with what we planned,' he exclaimed. 'We're going to have a baby. My beautiful, wonderful, adorable wife is going to have a baby!'

And the whole island is going to know about it in ten minutes flat, Jess thought ruefully, seeing Wattie Hope shoot back into the village hall as quickly as he'd come out, having clearly heard Ezra's every word.

'I don't care.' Ezra beamed when she told him. 'I *want* the whole island to know. I want the entire *world* to know. Oh, Jess, have I told you lately how much I love you?'

'You have.' She chuckled.

'And I'm never going to stop saying it,' he said softly, gathering her into his arms. 'Not to you, and not to our baby, because you and this island have given me everything I've ever wanted.'